THE YEAR OF THE OLD GOATS

Best wishes
[illegible]
10.5.95

"Goats alive! ...a paean of praise to the Senior golfer. A pleasure to read and wryly written." *JOHN HOPKINS. The Sunday Times.*

"It's bloody funny! It's just how the Seniors play, all over the place!" *W. WILTSHIRE. Professional, Bramshaw Golf Club.*

"...from a future 'Old Goat', my best wishes..." *TOM WATSON.*

"... a fine book and an entertaining one." *A recent winner of the U.S. MASTERS.*

"... gave me immense enjoyment... Golf is supposed to be fun. In this super-tale of the Old Goats the author has made it so... Great stuff!... and it's very well done." *PETER ALLISS.*

"... highly amusing... deserves exposure... readers will identify with the characters..." *DAVID WHITE in Through The Green, (June 1987), journal of The British Golf Collectors Society.*

"The six central characters of the novel are gentle and affectionate portrayals of the original Old Goats — Senior golfers who represent 'the stiffening backbone of golf'." *CATHARINE HUTTON in Trident (May 1987), journal of the Liverpool Chamber of Commerce.*

"... a charming book. A warm and amusing tale of golfers whose seniority is only exceeded by their enthusiasm... what makes the book rich and enjoyable is the depth of character in each of the leading players... flowing and descriptive narrative contrasting well with the often pithy dialogue. This is a study well worth your attention." *ALAN BENNETT in The Bucks Herald.*

"... a very neat and inviting format, and a very sunny, genial read." *JOHN RUTHERFORD.*

"Good old goat book. Will delight the golf fraternity... a funny book but a gentle book too." *The Stratford Herald.*

"... A goat among the birdies! The core of many a golf club, the Seniors have found at last a voice of sympathy... a humorous and affectionate homage... the breakthrough that brings respectful recognition for the Old Goats of the game." *T.F. in the Southport Visitor.*

"... the funniest golf novel for years."

THE YEAR OF THE OLD GOATS

by

GEORGE F. KERR

Illustrated by
Brian Alldridge

MOORE BOOKS

Reprinted July 1987.

Typeset/Design
Litharne, Long Marston, Warwicks

Printed in Great Britain by
The Herald Press, Stratford-upon-Avon, Warwicks

Published by
Moore Books, 38 Brook Street, Aston Clinton,
Aylesbury, Bucks HP22 5ES

ISBN 0 9511775 0 8

For
DONALD
who 'hit the drink' in 1941 in a Blenheim

and for
JOHN
who found deep rough in 1985.

The writer acknowledges a great debt to the original Old Goats, the true authors of this affectionate novel.
In real life, the Canadian was played by Tom Ellis, the Pilot by John Worth, the Nigerian by Jimmy Banks, the Swede by Eric Valgren and the Treasurer by Bernard Annetts.
The book attempts to measure and repay the friendship and companionship of marvellous hours on and off many a golf course.
Bill Livingstone, Captain of the club where some of the scenes are set, was the first real golfer to read the script and encourage the author in the belief that on every tee, green and fairway a number of players, similarly advanced in years and retarded in handicaps, would recognise and rejoice in the afflictions of these Old Goats.

Above all, the book is for
RUTH and CATHARINE

Chapter One

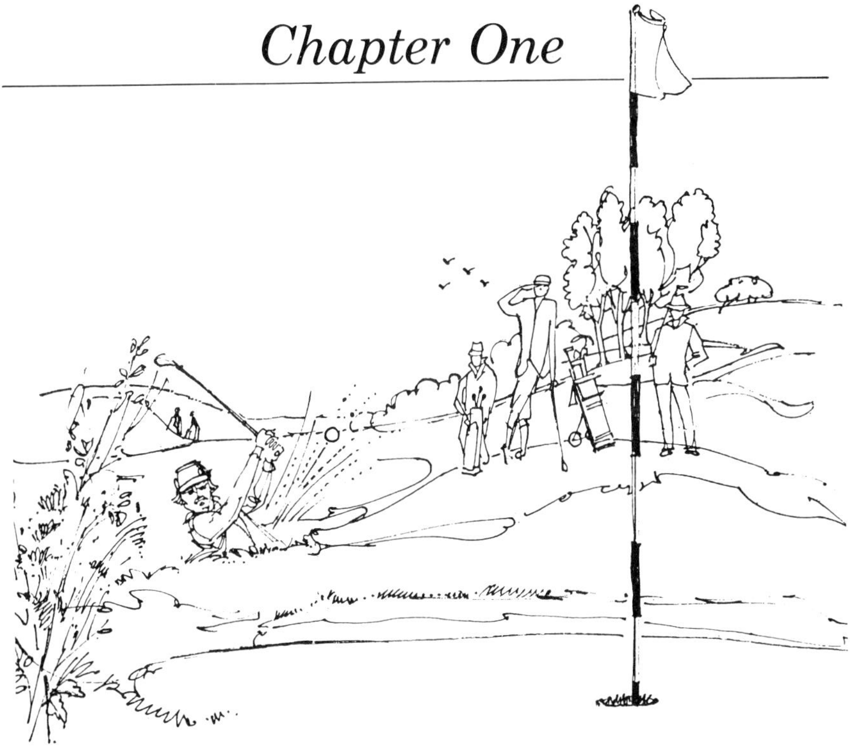

The Old Goats play the final hole

They moved slowly down the 9th hole six abreast. They fanned out across the breadth of the course, from the hedge and ditch to the west, where two of them were searching for their balls, across to the high bank to the east where the really long grass was and, ankle-deep in it, a third flailing figure. The head of a fourth player just showed over a fairway bunker, a hundred yards from the raised green. Two others stood patiently by their balls in the middle of the fairway.

The rest of the course was empty, for it was Tuesday morning and the other members of the club were at work. It wasn't one of your exclusive, up-market golf clubs. It was as humble and unpretentious in style as a village cricket club, and as fanatically focussed on its sport.

A fine drizzle had gently soaked them throughout their nine-hole round, but this had failed to dampen their zest, for today was the high point of their golfing calendar, the Old Goats' Open.

In the Pro.'s shop there had been twenty minutes of high-pressure salesmanship from the golf club Rep., and some good-natured customer resistance from the Pro. The Rep. could let him have forty sets of custom-tailored clubs as a pre-season 'snip'. Also a gadget for measuring a golfer's swing, length of arm and pivotal balance. The Rep. had recently taken a big order for the gadget from Gleneagles, Troon and Royal Birkdale. Could one of the smaller clubs afford to be out of the mainstream of golfing progress?

"We're not quite in the Gleneagles league" the young Pro. pointed out.

The Rep. was about to dispute this, as he thought, mock modesty, when his eye was caught, through the shop window, by the players he now noticed coming up the 9th. He counted them to himself. Six. He re-counted. Yes, six. In all his experience he had never seen a six-some playing a round together.

"It's the Old Goats' Open," the Pro. explained. "By special dispensation. They're a sort of club within a club. They're not young," he added, as though this explained everything.

The Rep. had to agree that they were not young.

"But they're keen."

The Rep., who himself played off a mean seven handicap, lit a cigarette and studied the golfers. The man on the hilltop had just sent his ball scudding and bounding diagonally across the course. Unchecked by the rough framing the ditch on the left, his ball disappeared into it.

"He's in the ditch. Mind you, with an action like that there was nowhere else the ball *could* go!" The Pro. joined him at the window.

"I've given them a few lessons. Some of them." He wasn't prepared to say which of them were his pupils. Sometimes he thought of them as his patients and, like any decent doctor, he wasn't going to betray professional confidences.

The next moment the bunker exploded and clods of wet sand urged the ball out of the trap. Meanwhile the two men on the fairway hit their balls in the general direction of the flag, the first with a high wedge shot to the shoulder of the green from which it was perversely shrugged off to the wrong side of a greenside bunker. The other man's shot was more deliberate. First there were two practice swings, then a little ritual with the grip of the hands, finally a rather stiff-armed blow which took the ball by surprise. It shot with some speed from the club, skimmed the surface of the green and hit the flag pin, ricocheting off it to a point ten yards from the green.

"Who are these guys?" the Rep. demanded with much the same

mixture of curiosity and dread that Butch Cassidy had shown for his pursuers. To the Pro. they were as unmistakeable, as individual in bearing, walk and address as, on the wider scene of world golf, were Nicklaus, Watson, Ballesteros and Trevino, their juniors by some thirty odd years. But the Pro. felt a certain loyalty to them. Why should this snooty Rep. try to suggest that simply because it wasn't being played on some snob course in Florida or Scotland the game the Old Goats were engaged in wasn't really golf? Of course it was the same game. Or very nearly the same. He studied the six members as they converged on the putting area, some dragging their trolleys, others favouring the lighter-built tripods.

WHO ARE THESE ELDER STATESMEN?

The Canadian, whose ball had hit the shoulder of the green, had now set off after it with the single-minded intent of a trapper after bear, his head forward in concentrated aggression, his trolley dragging after him like a sleigh through the snow-bound Rockies. He had the faculty of obliterating from his mind all thoughts save that of the lie of his ball.

It was the Swede who executed the shot from the long grass so much scorned by the Rep. Certainly the ball had travelled across the fairway diagonally, but he had at least hit it, and that was the object of the game surely. Now he made the hazardous descent into the fairway.

He had some difficulty in walking erect. His upper half would progress ahead of his feet, so that his lower limbs were often scuttling to catch up with his head. Downhill, the difficulty must have been greater, although he had never actually fallen forward on his face. But clearly it added problems to his game, which he found taxing enough, his eyesight not being all it might have been. He was not in fact a Swedish national, but he had remote Scandinavian connections, including a reception in years past at the Swedish Embassy where he had met King Gustav for three minutes over a sherry and a smorgasbord sandwich. The Canadian had once gently suggested that perhaps the Swede lost so many balls because of imperfect sight, but the Swede had disputed this. He had, he claimed, 20/20 distance vision. He spurned too the suggestion that his far-sightedness might be causing him problems in locating the ball on its tee. He had also been known to dispute his age. He was not 72! He was 71. Nor indeed did he look it, except that his eyes had the misty blue of an old sheepdog. He made his way across the fairway to the ditch. At this time of year it was not so much a ditch as a brook, even a small tormented rivulet.

The man who had exploded from the bunker was the County Treasurer. The shot spattered his face with wet sand, but he was quietly satisfied with it. The others all had high expectations prior to making their shots; whereas the Treasurer was always quietly certain that whatever the particular golf problem facing him he would fail to solve it. He obviously knew, as a statistician, what the odds were against him and welcomed therefore the occasional small successes of his game. This was by contrast with the deep and frequent bouts of despair into which his colleagues would plunge. Now, as he wiped the sand from his face and paced out the ten strides to his next shot, he grinned happily. It was a constant source of surprise to the others that the Treasurer seemed so much less affected by disaster than they.

He was additionally happy that he was not one of three players in the group required to mark the cards that day. The official markers were those who had, over the year, demonstrated an adequate standard of numeracy. In the County Treasurer's Department there had always been batteries of computers, calculators and word processors available as well as a loyal staff, and he had successfully presided over their skilled analytical work. But the weighting of handicaps, the determination of how many strokes the Pilot must give to the Swede over nine holes and the rapid calculation of Stableford points — these niceties were beyond him.

"That's one of yours," the Rep. remarked as another shot was played.

"One of my what?"

"You've been giving him a lesson or two. I can tell. It's gone too far, that's all."

The Pilot's ball had indeed been a little strong. It had gone through the green and was heading for the car park. The Pilot when he reached the green, expecting to find his ball decently reposing on the flat sward found instead that it had crossed the putting surface and had stopped just short of the tarmacadam area. It was in a playable position but the Pilot scooped it up with his club and walked on towards the clubhouse, whistling soundlessly through pursed lips. He was writing this hole off.

The Pilot had flown Sunderlands during the war. Now almost forty years later he drove his souped-up Ford Cobra as though it were a war plane. He couldn't bear to have another car on his tail. Nor could he tolerate any directly ahead of him on the road. To those unlucky enough to be his passengers it seemed that his car was not powered by the usual internal-combustion engine but by a phalanx of booster rockets slung beneath the car's undercarriage. Between boosts the Pilot's eyes would hood in the boredom of a steady 75mph. It then came as a relief for another vehicle to drop back to them on the motorway for the Pilot would be fully awake again and spurting past the offender.

His golf too was rocket-assisted. There would be spasms of successful shots followed by the tedium of shanks, hooks and misputts. During the war he had never thought of quitting his Sunderland in self disgust. On the golf course he knew when enough was enough, when to pick up as now on the verge of the car park, and wander off towards the clubhouse to await the others.

He was good at cutting his losses. Towards the end of a particularly unsuccessful hole, while the others were still footling around on the green he was able to detach himself from the immediate problems of the round, and, hand on hip, stare about him at the landscape and the clouds scudding overhead or at a young crow, twice the size of its mother, bullying her out of her mind for more worms or whatever she could find in the rich semi-rough. He waited patiently now for the five others to complete their rounds, and marvelled at the peace of the scene.

No doubt at this very moment cabinet meetings were being held and company planning sessions. Men were repairing cars or tending chocolate-wrapping machines as if their lives depended on it. In the Sudan thousands were dying of starvation. In Pakistan some freedom fighters had hijacked a Boeing. Surgeons were stitching up stomachs. Crooks were plotting a bank raid. Kids were converting centimetres to millimetres. Priests were hearing confessions. Teeth were being pulled out. Frauds were being 'rumbled'. Men and women were considering adultery or adoption or marriage. People were dying quietly. Others were giving birth. But here close to the 9th, his friends were moving gently towards the conclusion of yet another nine holes. And the monster baby of a crow was demanding of its distracted mother yet more worms to stifle its 'caw' and ease its terrible hunger.

The Treasurer and the Canadian were still waiting for the other three. The Swede had pushed his way through the bushes by the brook in his search for his ball. The Actor and the Nigerian were considering crossing to the brook to help him find it.

"By the time we get there," the Nigerian reasoned, "he'll either have found it or have given it up and be playing another."

"I can't see him," the Actor said. "It must be actually in the water."

'There he is."

They could see his head and shoulders. He was holding on to a bough. Then there was a loud crack as the bough snapped off, and the Swede's head disappeared from sight.

"There is a willow grows aslant a brook," the Actor said.

"Do you think he's gone in?"

"He's only got to keep his head above the surface. He'll be all right."

"What happened?" the Nigerian shouted.

"I expect an envious sliver broke," the Actor said.

They had crossed towards the brook when they saw his head reappear.

"He's all right."

In fact he was soaking. He had fallen right into the fast moving water and when they reached him he was still sitting there, like Eeyore, the brook babbling past his waist, his hat floating away merrily downstream.

"Give us a hand," the Swede said and the Actor yanked him out. The Nigerian meanwhile had given chase and recaptured the hat. It too was dripping.

The Rep. had watched this with some astonishment.

"I saw Langer go up that tree at Fulford and play it from there," he said. "And who was it took his shoes off and played it barefoot out of the lake at the Masters? But this really takes the bloody cake."

"It's certainly different," the Pro. agreed.

"They're playing on!" the Rep. said.

"Of course they are! It's their Open. They don't give up just for a bit of casual water. Not this lot."

The Nigerian indeed was now playing his third shot to the green. But he hit it 'thin' and sent the ball through and beyond the green after a glancing contact with the pin. The Swede was dripping water all over the fairway and his shoes and socks were squelching as he sloshed after the others.

The 'Nigerian' was so called because of his twenty years spent in the White Man's Grave of West Africa. He had been overseas controller of all vehicles belonging to the multinational conglomerate which he had served loyally and well since the war. Silver headed now and silver moustached, the Nigerian, who was of course as white as the ace of diamonds, still produced the neat, economical swing taught him by his father back in the Twenties. This was not always as well grooved as it had been in the past. Compact and neat in style, he was the Old Goats' Trevino to the Canadian's Arnold Palmer, cunning opposed to brute force.

Not that the Old Goats saw themselves in the professionals' clothing. They were, at least overtly, humble and unpretentious about their golf.

But secretly, some of the masters' colour had rubbed off on each of them. The Swede, for example, affected a right-hand glove flapping at his hip pocket, in the manner of Palmer. None of them would have thought of pushing a shopping trolley round a supermarket wearing the hat he favoured for golf. On suitable occasions, like a Mixed Doubles, the Pilot and the Actor would appear in plus twos, the one in sombre tweed, the other in the tartan of the Black Watch. The Canadian, though, eschewed any such fancy dress. He was dressed and equipped for the bear hunt and that was an end to it. Except that he bore on his waterproofs a logo which recorded oil research in Canada by British Petroleum back in the sixties, of a glaring orange shade which ensured his safety should he find himself at dusk looking for his ball on the nearby main road.

"Play every day, do they?" the Rep. asked.

"Ten every morning. All weathers."

"But do they get any better?"

The Pro. didn't much care for the tone of the Rep.'s questions.

"Do you reckon this gadget of yours would do their pivotal balance any good?"

"We've had no complaints from the clubs that *have* taken it on. The Belfry, Mellion, Sandwich..."

"Ah, but this isn't Sandwich, is it?"

"I tell you what. I'll leave it with you, sale or return. Take that old chap there, for instance. Shafts too long. Pivotal balance all to hell. He's using the wrong clubs, that's all there is to it!"

They watched as the Actor played his approach shot. Then he crossed to join the Nigerian and they seemed to be comparing scores on their cards. They played their own slightly complicated game which involved Stableford points. This of course didn't affect the Canadian, or the Swede.

There had been several futile attempts to instruct the Canadian in Stableford, and the Swede, accident-prone in so many aspects of the game, always came to the contest equipped with a ballpoint pen which had run out of fluid or a broken stub of a pencil. The Actor, while 'resting' between engagements, had read all the available books on both golf and mathematics. Accordingly he had offered his services and had recruited in turn as markers the Pilot and the Nigerian. These three, therefore, took on the further burden of counting their colleagues' shots in addition to their own, thus freeing the Swede, the Treasurer and the Canadian to focus their attentions exclusively on their own tortured game, with special attention to grip, stance and swing.

The chief marker, the Actor, was self-appointed. If he had learned anything in life, in addition to approximately one-tenth of all the words written by Shakespeare, as well as some few by Chekhov and Coward, it was that most people when confronted by even simple figures and the sums involving them became light-headed. He was extremely intolerant of folly, defined in his mind as the inability to remember how many strokes A should receive from B, A playing off 15, B off 21 and the handicap allowance being established as three quarters of the difference. It was the Actor therefore who made out all the cards for the Old Goats; if some players, off 28, were lucky enough to receive two strokes at certain holes and one each at the remainder, these digital figures were meticulously recorded by the Actor for the guidance of his retarded playing companions. And whereas other players could be temporarily distracted by the sound of a tripod collapsing to the ground exactly at the top of their swings, the Actor's game could be ruined for weeks if the man supposed to be recording the Actor's score suddenly confessed that he had forgotten to record any score for anyone at the 12th, and here they were at the 18th tee with apparently two holes still to play!

The fact that the Actor could not have built a go-cart for his grandson as had the Nigerian, out of a shopping basket and a thin-wheeled trolley, or that he would not have known which way to face if invited to fly a Sunderland, as the Pilot had for four years in and out of flak, that he was in fact, mechanically speaking, an imbecile did not in any way modify his deep scorn for the mathematically less gifted.

There was a quid pro quo about this arrangement. The Actor's grandson received out of the blue a seemingly new go-cart for Christmas from an unknown Nigerian, and at least three of the six Old Goats who had not been known to make a calculation in their lives since decimalisation, astonished their wives by their unsuspected skills in golfing arithmetic. It was the Actor too who had initiated for the Old Goats their own handicapping system, based on each nine holes played throughout the year. This fine calculation involving decimal points was ahead of its time and of any recommendations by the Royal and Ancient authorities in St. Andrews. It ruled out altogether the movement of handicaps upwards, and the Actor was only outvoted to general uproar when he suggested that in the cause of even greater accuracy, the handicaps should be assessed to two decimal places. An offer of a calculator to affix to his trolley was rejected by the Actor with contempt. They were all agreed, surely, that the game of golf took place 'up here', and he touched with his finger the seat of his brain. So, he maintained, did scoring.

THE OLD GOATS' OPEN

The Old Goats' Open was in fact exclusive to the six founder members. It was to be played over nine holes and at each hole there would be, as well as Stableford points, Stableford putting points too — three points for a single putt, two for two putts and one for three. There were two points for 'nearest the pin' at the short hole, two points for the longest drive at the long 8th. And on the par four holes, two points for reaching the green in the regulation two shots. Additionally, and there were murmurs when the Actor announced this, there were to be three bonus awards, whose nature was concealed in an envelope in which the Actor's wife had set out the basis for the bonuses. This envelope would be opened at the conclusion of the nine holes, with consequent adjustments made in the final placings.

The Actor swore that he was not privy to the contents of this envelope. It might be, he suggested, that anyone with white hair or a sketchy knowledge of Swedish could be docked six points. Or that twelve bonus points would be added to the count of anyone who had ever played the part of Horatio on the stage.

The Pilot had reached the clubhouse and had turned to watch from a distance his five competitors finish their rounds. They were all safely on the green and now they gathered to inspect the prospect of their final putts. From where the Pilot stood, the solemn little group had the appearance of five eye witnesses to a minor street accident, standing motionless over the corpse of a cat. Then one of them took a respectful pace forward, then another, the Swede, bending now with some difficulty and taking his ball from the hole. The others followed in their turn. After each stroke, the small group shuffled a little and then re-formed and was still again. It was, from that distance, as though each had to bend and touch the cat, in tribute to its shortened life. Ten handshakes followed and the little ritual came to its end with the slow march back to the clubhouse, their trolleys dragging behind them.

In the changing room, as mudded golf shoes were shed and they struggled purple-faced out of their waterproofs, questions formed in their minds but were not put. Who had won? Had the Pilot picked up at the 9th? But conversation proper was reserved for the comfort and relaxation of the club room. The Swede was busily making a complete change of clothing. Finally they were all clean and in their normal clothes once more and the changing room was heaped with piles of pullovers and funny hats and left-hand gloves. They all agreed however to the Canadian's suggestion that they would have the usual. The scorecards, duly signed and countersigned, had been handed to the Actor, and they repaired to a table with six glasses on it and before going any further drank deep.

Each old Goat had been asked to contribute the cash equivalent of one and a half golf balls towards the prizes. Only the Canadian had failed, till then, to cough up. Of Fundamentalist-Scots ancestry, he would never play for money, as a matter of principle. The Actor took it upon himself to satisfy the Canadian's conscience.

"You don't have to put in money," he pointed out. "You can contribute a ball and a half, if you would prefer that."

"Why a ball and half?"

It was back to elementary Maths again.

"Because," said the Actor, "there are six of us. Six times 1½ makes 9. The winner gets three balls, the runner-up two and everyone else..."

"... loses half a ball each?"

"... gets a ball as compensation," the Actor concluded.

"Oh, I get it," the Canadian said, but without any conviction, and paid the levy. Nine yellow balls were then brought in from the Professional's Shop, and the judging began. There was a brief dispute over the long drive. Was the Treasurer's drive on the fairway or not? Five votes for semi-rough, one, the Treasurer's, for fairway. The Treasurer lost and the Pilot had gained himself two points.

The measurement of two rival balls on the short hole had filled twenty happy minutes in their round. The Swede had paced out one of the balls, the Nigerian the other. Nineteen paces, according to the Swede. The Nigerian made it twenty three. Objection! The Nigerian being a small man had taken more paces but shorter ones. The Nigerian was therefore replaced by the Pilot who was invited to re-measure the two balls, this time using the toe-and-heel technique. Fifty nine shoe lengths was his verdict and the winning points went to the Swede.

There had been only one successful reaching of the par four greens in a regulation two. As for the putting tourney, there had been a quantity of three-putts and the Actor had two-putted five times. He awarded himself ten Stableford putting points. The Treasurer also claimed ten, including four tremendous points as a result of chipping in at the 7th hole.

"If one putt earns three points, no putts must receive four!" he pointed out.

The other five went into temporary shock at this, but reference to the Rules of Golf was not helpful to their case. The Stableford points had been distributed amongst them fairly evenly. It was simply a question now of addition, after which they could open the mystery envelope. They solemnly passed their cards round and each battled with the handwriting idiosyncracies of his colleague. Finally it emerged that the Canadian was in the lead, with the Pilot second, the rest nowhere, particularly the Swede and the Nigerian, respectively last and next to last. The Actor opened the envelope.

"First bonus" he read. "The last shall receive six extra points as compensation."

This meant that the Swede at once jumped into fifth place, ahead of the Nigerian, and this adjustment was loudly applauded by the Swede.

"Second bonus," the Actor continued. "To the player who sank the longest putt of the day, six extra points."

"Mine!" the Treasurer claimed in some excitement. "At the 7th. A beauty, it was!"

They all remembered the shot and they all disallowed it as a putt.

"You topped it!" said the Canadian.

"I may have topped it. I *meant* to top it. To give it the necessary roll."

"You topped it from off the green!"

"So?"

"So it wasn't a putt. And you've already had four points for it."

"That's mean and sneaky," the Treasurer complained.

"Sinking it at all was mean and sneaky."

It was finally decided that the Treasurer's shot be disallowed and that, by contrast, the Swede's putt at the 8th hole which had a certain freakish quality to it deserved the award. It had taken an S-course to the hole and then, hitting a small worm cast, had lunged awkwardly down.

"I'm catching you people up, aren't I? What's the next bonus?"

"The final bonus," the Actor read out, " is six points to any player under the age of 63."

A silence fell on the group. Some of them glanced at the Treasurer, the 'baby' amongst them.

"No one's got the nerve to claim six points for that, I take it? Right!" said the Actor. "Now the final score. The winner with thirty points ..."

He was interrupted by the Nigerian.

"Wait a bit! Who on your list is last?"

The Actor glanced at his paper.

"You are."

"Quite. So I receive six extra points."

"Which then puts *me* last," added the Swede, "and therefore I now claim a further six points."

"Out of order!" ruled the Pilot. "This is not a recurring bonus, ad infinitum."

"Agreed," the Actor ruled. "And on behalf of the Old Goats' Committee, I am happy to present the first prize to our friend from the Colonies."

Three balls were passed to the Canadian and two to the Pilot as runner-up. There was a round of applause and the Canadian rose to his feet.

"It's kind of nice to beat the Old Country at its own game. What'll you Imperialists have?" And he took their orders.

Chapter Two

How some of the Old Goats bravely battled with distressing physical disabilities, avoided unsuitable partnerships and banded together to improve their game

From time to time, the Old Goats operated their own Clinic, where minor imperfections in a member's play were given the sympathetic attention of the others. The Actor, who was somewhat bookish, tended to go for guidance to the written works of Jack Nicklaus. He approved of the colour illustrations to the Nicklaus text. Although he wouldn't have been found dead with a strip cartoon open in his lap, he didn't put these instructive pictures in the same category as 'Peanuts' or 'Popeye' for Nicklaus had not stooped to having bubbles coming out of his players' mouths.

Unfortunately, the faults afflicting the Old Goats' game were rarely touched on in the instructional books. The list of contents included many references to 'schlafing' and 'the yips', but there was never any mention, for example, of 'the staggers'. Yet the Nigerian clearly had intermittent bouts of this dread affliction. Indeed, on his first game ever with the rest of the Old Goats he had shown early symptoms of it. He had bent on the 1st tee to place his ball on its peg. There had been some trouble with the wind forcing its way under his loose-fitting sun-jack and disturbing his equilibrium. Perhaps too the tee was defective, for the ball refused to stay on it. Whatever the reason, he was down there for what seemed like minutes. The others had waited politely, but the Actor, sensing that they were witnessing a catatonic trance, or worse, hissed to the others:

"He's gone! I think he's gone!"

Slowly, the Nigerian had regained an upright position, his white locks and white moustache setting off the flushed pink of his face. Then the neat, grooved swing with which the others were soon to become so familiar sent the ball down the fairway in a stylish parabola to cover his one hundred and thirty five trouble-free yards. The shot received the applause it merited, and the Nigerian brushed his moustache upwards with the back of his hand.

In later months he was to confess that whereas he had expected a polite bonhomie from this veteran group which he would have been happy to take or leave, the mordancy he found in the badinage, the sweet-and-sour hail and farewell note in the words "I think he's gone!" quite endeared the Old Goats to him and, as far as golf was concerned, he was theirs for life.

His first few weeks at the club, he had found himself trapped in a regular four-ball with a married couple of advanced years and a German who had spent the war in a P.O.W. camp in the Lake District. It had been kind of them to invite him to join them although he soon found himself unhappy about their rate of play. They would take never less than twenty five minutes to each hole, most of the time spent in looking for balls, their own or other people's. They had all three had a number of lessons, but obviously the basic feature of the game had not been communicated. The spirit of the chase would send them happily off into the long grass from where they would only too gladly wave through pairs and fours moving conventionally up the fairway from tee to green.

If they made an early start at nine in the morning, they could be expected back in the clubhouse by a quarter to two. The Nigerian's wife found it hard to believe that much of this time had been spent looking for lost balls. Wasn't there a time limit for that? Yes. Five minutes. Then? Well, it was a friendly. A friendly? For nearly five hours? Anyway, how many had he gone round in? Fifty eight. Fifty eight? But that's marvellous. For nine holes. Nine! Christ!

How the German had been taken prisoner by the Allies emerged bit by bit, or divot by divot, for he was a savage player.

"Ich haben heet die graund agehn!" he would say in a guttural statement of the obvious. He hadn't fought in Africa. He hadn't been part of the all-conquering Reich troops sweeping through the Low Countries to the Channel ports in '40. Where had he been taken then? It was a difficult subject to broach with a former enemy, now engaged in sabotage of one of the U.K. fairways.

In fact he had been an electrician unluckily repairing fuses when Goering had ordered the Luftwaffe to an immediate blitz on Warwick Castle in October 1939. Crossing the Thames, the plane he was a passenger on, although an unwilling one, had developed further electrical faults. The crew, believing their number was up, had generously tossed him a spare parachute and persuaded him to jump. Then the fault had righted itself and his companions had returned safely to Hamburg. The German had parachuted to earth in front of the Luton Town Hall, and a taxi driver had picked up this unexpected fare and delivered him to the nearest police station.

There was the danger, the Nigerian had sensed, that he might be playing the same four-ball, Tuesdays and Thursdays, for life. Discreetly he changed his playing days to Wednesdays and Fridays and put a neatly typed cry for help on the club notice board.

'Ex-overseas member, good standard of golf, seeks congenial playing companion. Ring...'

The Canadian responded to this agony call and the five Old Goats became six. Subsequently, when they compared notes, the Actor, who had also been a prisoner of war for five years in Bavaria, recalled an occasion in the clubhouse when the German, made bold perhaps by several glasses of Guinness, had been complaining about the length of his prison sentence. He had spent six years behind the wire in a remote camp near Wastwater.

"It's a very pretty part of the country," the Actor said. "Besides," he added, "your lot started it."

Amazingly, the German had disputed this. The British, it seemed, were responsible for World War II. Because of their treaty with Poland, the British had declared war.

"We should have fought on the same side," the German told his listeners. "Together we would have been the masters of Europe."

The Old Goats, who had long ago put away their khaki and their Air Force blue uniform showed decent restraint at this, unwilling to put the boot into a former wearer of field grey. Instead they shuffled their feet and hoped the subject would change.

Some weeks later, the Actor came across the German by the 3rd tee. The German was about to drive from it, and the Actor stood at a safe distance to one side to watch, before chipping to the 2nd green. The German's drive sliced off sixty degrees to the right and the ball whizzed past the Actor's ear.

"Ich haben heet die graund agehn" the German said in what the Actor took for a Teuton's apology.

"Not to worry," he said lightly. "I can think of worse places to die than a golf course!"

"Vorse places? Like what?"

"Well, like a gas..." He bit back the words. It was, after all, a cloudless day. All was well with the world — now. Or with this patch of it. The sun on the back of his neck persuaded him to silence, but when he came to the 3rd tee, and saw the German ahead of him on the left of the fairway, he hit his drive with a venomous thwack that remembered each of his five years in the hands of the enemy.

And so the Nigerian had joined the merry company of Old Goats, but look as they might they could find no mention of his disability in the works of Peter Alliss or John Jacobs or Tom Watson. The dictionaries all noted that sheep suffered from the staggers. But since this was of no immediate help, there stemmed from this omission the Old Goats' Clinic, at which the combined play-experience of all could come to help solve the problems of one of their number.

Each of them, it emerged, had had experience at some time of this transient, ovine affliction, grave in sheep, trivial, they all assured him, in man. It was caused, roughly, by blood rushing to the head and then rushing away from it. The brain suddenly starved of the stuff, could do no less than send its dizzy alarm message. You could experience the same symptoms by stooping too long to read the titles of books in the lower shelves at the Public Library or, if you were of a mechanical turn, by trying to peer under the car at the sump case or the big end.

They all benefited from this pooling of symptoms, for they were relieved to find that they shared such phenomena as occasional double vision, breathlessness on approaching the raised 6th green, and allergic reaction to pollen during the dry months or to black cats crossing the fairway.

The Nigerian and the Canadian both had 'puffers', Ventolin inhalers to control their breathing in stressful moments, for they were both chronic sufferers from asthma and/or emphysema. Luckily these moments of stress occurred for the most part round the pool table after the golf, when laughter at some fluke stroke would send them bent and reeling from the table. The Canadian, modelling his play on his compatriot Kirk Stevens rather than the more sedate Cliff Thorburn, would free himself from a snooker by a shot that would rocket round the table and end up with a four-cushion pot of a ball he hadn't even noticed. The others would watch fascinated as the two 'puffers' were whipped out and resuscitative draughts of neat oxygen, or whatever the healing gas was, were rushed to the deprived lungs.

Several of them were on tablets too. The Nigerian had swallowed six thousand of them that year, of various shapes and colours. The Canadian admitted to being on steroids, and there was a move by the other four, on the eve of the Old Goats' Open, to submit both players to a urine test. This was ruled against on aesthetic grounds; it would be too messy to administer and no one was sure how to test the specimens.

There were a number of other ailments lightly skirted over by the group; skirted over because each of them felt his clinical condition to be a matter of confidence between himself and his medical adviser. The Pilot's thyroid trouble seemed to be well under control. It was this that had led him to take up golf once more after an absence of thirty years from the game. The Pilot's wife had mentioned to the wife of the Canadian that all was not well. Moods of depression. Listlessness. Apathy. The Canadian, for his part, found himself re-reading the Sun all morning and this too had been a depressant. The idea came to him that he and the Pilot might better enjoy their mornings away from their armchairs and swinging a club. And so it came about, and the double depression was at once dispersed.

From time to time, one of the six would be missing for a day.

"Just having his six-month check up," a colleague would report. And the following day this missing member would be greeted by the others as dogs would rush to muzzle and sniff one of their pack, released to them from the back seat of a hot saloon car.

No heavy questions like "What did the quack say about you?" or "How long did he give you?" It was good to have him back. Let's toss for partners. Your honour.

Emphysema and the like do not appear in the Nicklaus instructional works. It was thus up to the Old Goats' own Clinic to handle such issues, which they did. They ignored them. But the gravest symptom the Clinic was ever called to deal with resulted from the very effects of instruction.

One of the group would occasionally go to the Pro. for an hour's tutorial. The Pro., a stripling of some twenty summers, was, it was generally agreed, a nice chap and a first rate teacher. He didn't bully or flatter and he was able to keep his face straight however grotesque the shot offered for his critical comment. Inevitably, though, he would suggest that 'something had to be done about that grip'. Either the fingers of the left hand were too far under the club or too far over. Whichever it was, the cure was the same, a fundamental reshaping of every digital positioning learned or acquired over the last thirty or forty years, and practised on golf courses in every corner of the world.

The effect on the pupil was traumatic. It was heartbreaking to see one's friend and colleague twisting his gnarled hands into convulsions as he tried to put into practice what he had learned the previous day. The others were deeply moved to see their companion who two days ago could be relied upon to send the ball scudding from the tee all of 120 yards along the fairway, or slightly to the right of it into the semi-rough, now contorting himself desperately to hit the ball at all. A man playing off a consistent 28 now found himself, after one lesson, in the Ladies 36 (Provisional) category. During these initial agonies the others held their peace. Soon they found themselves muttering the futile encouraging words of the doctor: "If you persevere with the regime I have given you, I think you will get some relief."

It was like consoling a wounded animal. The eyes of the sufferer would turn towards them in stricken hope. The agony lasted about a week, then it was over. Either the patient had 'thrown physic to the dogs' and secretly returned to his bad old ways, gripping the club as he had always gripped it and what the hell! Or else, miraculously, the cure had begun to work. The lift of the ball was better, the direction better and he had gained all of ten yards in distance. The whole driving game was infinitely improved. Except that, alas, the price to be paid for this blessing seemed to be that around the green, suddenly, all was ineffectual disaster and a new despair.

The passing of the old grip would be silently mourned in the same mood as would have been the recent death of a colleague's elderly aunt. But new problems arose, and the Clinic was kept busy throughout the year. The Treasurer would develop a tendency to 'heel' every fairway shot. The Canadian, while capable of holing putts of twenty feet and longer, seemed unable to deal successfully with a two-footer. Mysterious hooks and slices appeared from nowhere, like a plague of stinging ants, and the player would be driven, in extremis, to declare in ringing tones that certainly there was no God.

The Swede, walking in from the 9th hole, would confide in the Actor that "Today my short game went altogether." This greatly surprised the Actor who hadn't realised, till then, that the Swede had ever had a short game. He had always thought that between drive and putt the Swede generally practised his own Scandinavian form of hockey. Perhaps he had, on this round, delivered half a dozen more blows than usual, but once they approached double figures who was counting?

In any case the Swede brought some of his high-scoring problems on himself. He was inordinately attached to his woods and insisted on using them in the most unsuitable lies. If his ball was in long grass, as it generally was, and fairly well embedded at that, he would hope to punch it out with a 3 wood, but not in the general direction of the fairway where he might expect to get some well-earned relief. More often he would send it hopping a few yards deeper in, as might a frog being harried by a baseball bat.

The others, by now on the green, would await his arrival like an explorer gaining a clearing in the jungle, a little breathless from his exertions, his triumphant 3 wood still ready in his hand. They would hesitate to ask him how many he was to there. They left it to him to give them the final figure, as the ball ended its long journey to the hole.

"It's my short game that's letting me down," the Swede would say philosophically and plod after the others to a further test of it at the next hole.

HOW THE OLD GOATS DEALT WITH EUPHORIA, DESPAIR AND THE PERILS OF NATURE

One of the problems most frequently brought to the attention of the Clinic was that of Address. All the experts were agreed, as indeed were the Old Goats, that the position of a player's feet in relation to that of the ball was critically important. A common snap judgement on some pathetic mishit could be: "Standing too close to the ball!" or alternatively "Not standing close enough!", the two conflicting diagnoses entering the offender's separate ears. There then followed the almost metaphysical problem of the Ideal Distance or, as the Greeks probably knew it, the Golden Stance.

Various theorists of the game would describe to avid readers of the golfing monthlies the most suitable position in which the body should be held when contemplating a motionless ball. These articles were illustrated, according to the whim of the artist, either by matchstick figures in the manner of L.S. Lowry or by anatomical sketches after Leonardo where curiously shaped muscles would interweave in complex patterns. Occasionally the artist, no doubt a Rembrandt man, would forget the instructional side of his task and deliver to the surprised editor of the paper what was indubitably an Old Master; a lined, care-worn face studying a ball nestling in a lie of clover. Making the best of things, the editor would then ascribe a doubtful attribution: 'Tom Morris at the Road Hole, St. Andrews, 1879.'

The consensus view was that for the ideal stance, the player should allow his head to loll forward on his chest, his body to slump, knees bent, bottom extended, the whole configuration that of a collapsed S-shape, the extended club ensuring that the player remained precariously poised for his shot. That club extension, the pundits declared, should determine the optimum distance of ball from feet. More earthy experts likened the stance to that of a female dog passing water, but this simile was generally frowned on.

It was not particularly helpful to ask a striker whether he 'felt comfortable like that', for the honest answer must be 'Certainly not. How could I?' Nobody watching Arnold Palmer crouched over a putt could have thought that golf had anything at all to do with comfort. No, the question of what was the ideal distance was as circular as 'how long is a piece of string?' Besides, an individual's shape and contour was a further complicating factor.

The Treasurer, in profile, had the air of a man riding a horse which smelt disagreeably. His knees were well bent as he held his head back, reaching for the ball with a long, distasteful stretch of arm and club. The Canadian who never delayed in playing his shots, would stalk his ball, sneaking up on it and clouting it before he had had time even to think of foot placement. The Pilot brooded on the problem a great deal. He was sure that he went through exactly the same routine each time he addressed the ball, placing himself, as he thought, at the same distance from it. The ball evidently thought otherwise, for the results were inconsistent to the point of being called random. The Actor tried not to think about the subject at all. They all knew well enough that the game of golf took place not on a green meadowland but in some lobal area above the eyes and forward from the ears. The essence of the game, therefore, was to keep this cranial playing ground as free as possible from perplexing thoughts.

It was here that the Actor persuaded the Old Goats to take their first tentative steps into golfing psychology. He listed for his own purposes a series of Unacceptable Thoughts which were never on any account to be allowed admittance into a player's mind.

Euphoria and, more often, its counterpart despair were wholly Unacceptable and must be banished forthwith. They had all experienced those idiot, flitting ideas that would swarm at the smallest provocation. A man had only to birdie a hole, fluke in two successive longish putts, chip into the hole from the bracken, for his mind to start buzzing with grandiose dreams — of completing the course with thirteen more pars, going round in a lifetime's best, winning the Monthly Medal, being chosen Most Promising Old Goat of the Year, or some such fantasy.

It was enough even for the thought: "I'm playing really quite well today", modest enough in all conscience, to linger a moment in the mind, for that blameless thought to affect the man's play and lead to anticlimax at the next hole, at the very next stroke often enough, for he would play a total boo-boo of a shot, leading to a seven or worse and to the ruin of an otherwise tolerable card.

But equally Unacceptable, in the Actor's view, was the despair that followed the seven. That too must be banished, although it was easier to recognise distracting thoughts than it was to drive them from the mind. The thought that 'the four ahead are the slowest in the history of the game', was totally Unacceptable, even if true, for it ruined concentration and could increase the blood pressure in a man's circulatory system. So with such thoughts as 'Why does that ass drive before we are out of range?', for it led inevitably to a close and unhealthy study of the offending player's ritual over his strokes, his braying laugh across two fairways or his outlandish dress sense.

In fact, most thoughts being irrelevant to the business in hand were Unacceptable. An extremely well-balanced golfer, so the Actor had decided, a man in total control of his emotions, could spare a moment whilst awaiting his turn to play, to appreciate the song of the lark, the drift of the cumulus clouds or, depending on the season, the gentle settling of snowflakes melting on his cheeks and brow. But even these seemingly innocent aspects of nature could invade the mind of a highly-strung golfer. The Canadian at the 3rd tee always looked warily at the roof of the pigeon loft before driving off. He had been considerably unsettled once at this tee when the entire flight had taken off at the same moment with a great whirring of wings just as he was on his downswing. He couldn't to this day recall what dread it was that had clutched at his heart, something demonic, the bats of hell perhaps. But the effect had been disastrous. He had topped his drive.

At this same bird-haunted tee there lived, over the adjoining wall, a solitary hen. To the others it was simply bad luck that when the Pilot's turn came to drive off, the hen would appear jerkily through the hedge and pick her fastidious way, stiff-legged, from left to right across the teeing area, wide-eyed past the Pilot's Dunlop 65, her awkward head movements those of a sufferer from torticollis. It wasn't, the others felt sure, that the Pilot saw the bird as an omen of ill luck at the hole, though this was the result unfailingly produced. It was a little unsettling though, even to an agnostic and one free of all superstitious dreads, particularly as it happened to him five times in the same season. It so affected the Pilot that he had seriously considered playing eight- or sixteen-hole rounds in future.

It was obvious, the Actor pointed out to the others, that even homing pigeons or stiff-necked hens could easily become Unacceptable Thoughts. The problem was what to do about them, and the Actor proffered a solution. The only two thoughts that could be deemed acceptable, just two and no more, were: "Where is my ball?", and "How do I play this next shot?" The past was gone. The future was illusory. The immediate present and that alone was what must exclusively occupy the mind of the truly balanced golfer.

THE FLIGHT OF A WEDGE AND THE FLOCK OF LITTLE PINK PIGS

It was not clear how faithfully the other Old Goats followed this counsel. But one could read their reactions to false or disappointing shots. The Nigerian was sometimes seen to take his club and make as though to snap it across his thigh. The Actor has been known to fling his sand wedge twenty yards in the air then attempt to catch it as it fell, as though overcome with high spirits. And he had a stroke all his own, nowhere referred to in any text-book, for it was of his own perfecting. It was used on the putting green immediately after three-putting for a six when it might have been a four. He would pick the ball from its hole, swing the putter at it one-handed as he tossed the ball a foot in the air and clout it backhand onto the next tee. If the Royal and Ancient had had any sense of equity in drafting their rules, that stroke successfully executed should have drawn to itself a special bonus whereby the score at the last hole would be amended from six to four.

The Canadian, a man of usually iron control, occasionally threw back to his Saskatchewan origins. "Stop! Stop, you sod!" he would bellow after his 6 iron pitch as his ball headed directly for, then well past, the flag. This outburst generally occurred at the opening hole, as though this decent, restrained man from across the Atlantic had to give vent, early in the game, to the capacity he knew he had within for hating his ball. That first explosion made, he seemed able to settle down calmly to his game, quietly recording a steady stream of fives.

The Treasurer, expecting always the worst, grinned in its face when it happened. But the others noted that as the game went on, the grin became more and more fixed, even manic. The Pilot had little truck with outward reaction. He knew when he was beaten, and when he was really beaten he picked up. Many of the Pilot's cards, had they been entered in club competitions, would have been marked: N.R. — No Return. That was the Pilot's way of rejecting the immediate past. He put it in his pocket.

The Swede dealt with Unacceptable Thoughts by not being aware of them. He hadn't the same disappointment to face as they in not hitting the fairway, for the fairway in the Swede's game barely existed. He walked much further than they did. He saw interesting parts of the course that they rarely visited. He found more balls — other people's — than the others. He disturbed a quantity of tiny wildlife, furred and feathered, in the hedges and ditches. At the end of a game he would be covered with burrs and these he would pick off his pullover carefully. Perhaps he even counted them. He was probably the keenest golfer of the six, though that title the others would dispute, and they greatly respected him for his application to the game. And whereas they were readily cast down by some imperfection in their game, he by contrast was overjoyed when he managed at last to get some half-decent drive away and was congratulated on it by the others.

"That was a good one," they would say, relieved at not having to look for it.

"It was, wasn't it?" he would agree happily, his face beaming. It was noticeable about the Swede's rounds that he liked to have formulated for himself, before they all gathered in the clubhouse, a summary of his morning's play.

"I wasn't getting them away off the tee as well as usual," he would explain. Or "I let myself down on the greens."

Nobody challenged these statements, and it was only when he threatened to take off into the realm of purest fantasy that a halt was called. They were all prone to fantasy. It took the form of a sentence beginning "If only -" and ending "I'd have been round in level fives." Out of charity the fantasy would be allowed to run for a sentence or two.

"If I hadn't topped my 4 wood at the long 8th and found the ditch, I'd have been on the green in four and down in six perhaps five." (Instead of his actual nine.)

"Yes, and over the hills," the others would add in chorus, "there would appear a lovely flock of little pink pigs!"

But this fallacy was evident in the words of the others too.

"If I hadn't had a ten at the 3rd...", "If I'd sunk all those gimme putts", "If that bloody fool hadn't shouted 'Fore!' just when I was coming through on my downswing...", "If those women hadn't stopped to chat about their shopping instead of clearing the green...". If all those things had come about or not come about, the world would be a different place and golf would long ago have surrendered its mystery never to be played again.

The realisation of this truth ended one fallacy only by expressing another. "Ah well," they would say happily, "it's only a game." Only a game! What nonsense that clearly was. To the Old Goats, golf was solemn ritual, half war half peace. Delight and lunacy in equal parts. But 'only a game?' Certainly not.

THE SWEDE THREATENS TO TAKE HIS HANDICAP TO THE HOUSE OF LORDS

They had been discussing their handicaps. Some of the Old Goats were full members of the club, but four of them were mid-week members only. Under the official handicap system, handicaps could only be reduced as the result of play in a Qualifying Competition. For mid-week members, the only such games were the ten mid-week medals in the year, the two months around Christmas being devoted to frivolous battles for turkeys and liqueur whisky.

"Work it out for yourself," the Swede said. "If I play five days a week, two hundred and fifty rounds a year, and only ten of them count towards reducing my handicap, what chance have I got of bringing it down?"

They were all quick to see that the odds against the Swede so honing his game, on one of the ten Wednesdays when the mid-week medal was at stake, as to produce a breathless 97 gross and come down to a handicap of 27 were mind-boggling, though they didn't say so.

"It is a bit daunting," the Pilot agreed. But he was playing off 22. His three mandatory rounds before being awarded any handicap at all had included one of 69 net which he now regarded as freakish. Although quietly pleased with his 22 status, he was gloomy about his prospects of beating anyone from such a figure. The Canadian by quiet application had clawed his way down to 21. The Actor who, because of his work or lack of it, played more than the others, Saturdays and Sundays included, had gravitated to 18. The Treasurer, the Nigerian and the Swede each playing off the maximum may have grumbled about it, but they were not easy to beat, particularly over nine holes, where they received four strokes from the Actor.

But even this weighting was not enough for the Swede. He wanted to know why he only received three-quarters of the difference of five strokes. Why only four, and not five? The Actor was not sure of the reason for this, but he put up a plausible case.

"I can only suppose," he said, "that over the years, the Royal and Ancient, basing their thoughts on the experience of generations of players all over the world, have concluded that the granting of the full difference between a lower and a higher handicap player would be unfair to the former."

"You mean," the Swede had asked, "that the three-quarters ruling was invented so that the lower handicap man would be more likely to win?"

"Yes," the Actor admitted, "that is what I mean."

"Well I don't agree with the ruling," the Swede said, and looked to the Nigerian and the Treasurer for moral support. This, naturally, was immediate, and the Actor realised that he had a potential rebellion on his hands.

"If you wish to overturn the entire framework of contemporary society by insisting on receiving the full difference, you will be setting your face against every decent concept within the game that our forefathers have laboured to secure for us. But you are fully entitled to take your case formally to St. Andrews. No doubt beyond that you have grounds of appeal through the civil courts and thence upwards to the House of Lords. I simply wish you the best of luck, that's all."

"All I am saying," the Swede insisted, "is that I should get five strokes from you over nine holes..."

"I know what you're saying."

"... and that these should be at the 2nd, 3rd, 4th, 8th and 9th."

"Look" the Actor said, "if Tom Watson, Henry Cotton, Bobby Jones, Harry Vardon and James Braid were to walk into this clubhouse now and be asked whether you should get a stroke from me at the 2nd and 9th, what the hell do you think they'd say?"

"They'd say it was a silly question."

"Quite! Because it is a silly question."

The impasse was broken by the Canadian, the man of peace at any price.

"I move that we leave it as it is" he said. The Pilot supported him.

"Well they would, wouldn't they?" the Treasurer pointed out. "They're the low handicap chaps, aren't they?"

"Only in relation to you three," the Pilot said. "When we play against someone off 15 *we* get only three-quarters of the difference. It's swings and roundabouts."

So it was agreed, and the three-quarters differential descended upon them again. It was this debate that brought about the Old Goats' own handicap system. The Actor would record every nine-hole score they returned and there would be adjustments in handicaps, daily if need be. No upward movements. Anyone beating their net score would be immediately chopped, in the case of the three higher handicap men by .2 per stroke, .1 in the case of the three others. The system had proved to be a success. From week to week they all either jumped or crept down the scale by decimal points, until only the Swede remained aloof and untouched on 28. The others patiently awaited the day when he returned a card showing a gross of 48, net 34 and a reduction in his handicap to 27.8. And on that day, they reflected, over the hills would appear a lovely flock of little pink pigs...

These casual, friendly encounters each day had seemed to the Actor too casual. There was not sufficient incentive offered for any of them to improve their play. The others were happy enough to humour the Actor as the 'Mad Ideas' man. This stemmed from the fact that the others had spent their lives mastering machinery or administering people; the Actor was a man who, at the drop of a hat, would stand on a table in the bar and sing or juggle for his supper. There was no suggestion that he could be expected to harbour an idea.

The Actor was of the opinion that their daily games needed an injection of 'show biz'. So they played their own Monthly Medal and Stableford, then a mixture of the two. Also a putting Stableford and a knockout match play and, in a grand combination of these, or as many of them as could be recorded on the normal scorecard, the Old Goats' Open. Over the months, the far wall of the changing room became posted with the running scores in these exclusive competitions, to the bewilderment of full-time members who wondered whether they were missing something.

DOMESTIC DISTRACTIONS AND CONSEQUENT ABSENTEEISM AMONG THE OLD GOATS

Not that they were an exclusive subgroup, although the Actor liked to refer to them, provocatively, as the Militant Tendency. Politically, of course, they were no such thing. Four of them were deepest blue in their attitudes, one was a golfing Socialist, the other a Lib-Lab man. In religious or quasi-religious terms, two were Anglicans, one a lapsed Catholic, one was a Freemason, one an agnostic and one an atheist. In the unreal world outside, events like the Falklands War, the Miners' Strike, the four million unemployed, the devaluation of the pound vis-a-vis the dollar, passed by with as little notice or comment as the French Revolution in Jane Austen's novels. There would be an occasional knee-jerk reaction to certain news items — England winning the third Test in Madras, the Brighton bomb, Terry Wogan's 40-foot putt in Celebrity Golf.

There were other claims on their time apart from golf. There were wives and children in the background, shopping demands, one or two jobs round the house, cars to be attended to: the antifreeze topped up or the headlights wiped clean of mud. The Pilot, when the fever struck him, would make early morning trips to the pits at Silverstone and spend the day there happily inhaling carbon monoxide during some smelly, noisy Grand Prix. The Swede was called on, at certain seasons of the year, to make excursions to Wisley and Spalding to inspect roses or tulips.

Brief reference would be made to a daughter, a silversmith crafting brooches for sale through Harrods to American tourists, another editing a dictionary for Collins and guiding other tourists round Stratford-on-Avon, a son who had got through to the Eastern Counties' Quarter Final in a War Games competition and yet another daughter who, only a few months into her marriage, found herself married to a paraplegic, the result of a car crash. There were unfair handicaps in life too. Grandchildren made occasional visits to the club where the most interesting feature for them seemed to be the row of urinals in the men's changing rooms.

They also appreciated the fruit machines and the investment made in them on their behalf by five of the six Old Goats. But by and large, glimpses of that outside world were rarely reflected within the clubhouse walls.

Some domestic chores the Old Goats found difficulty in shedding. The Gas Company figured large in the Canadian's 'other life' outside. His central heating system was always 'playing up' and he would make appointments with the man from the gas to check the system for him. He would stay confined to barracks for days at a stretch awaiting the man's arrival with his spanner and of course these enforced 'lay-offs' played havoc with his swing. The Nigerian requested leave of absence too to do some painting job in his sitting room, though the others felt that his wife, if she couldn't handle the job herself, might have earmarked it as an evening's chore, rather than during golfing hours.

It was never clear, though, what the Nigerian's free hours were. On soaking days, when golf was out of the question and the others would prepare to go their ways after a couple of frames of pool, the Nigerian would become quite miserable, glancing at the clock which showed 10.40. He had, he said, about four hours to kill, for if he got home at 11 instead of 2.30 he might be expected to get back at that time every day he played. It was suggested that he might hide in the Public Library for a couple of hours, but he was reluctant to do this. On the other hand, when his wife was away visiting a daughter in London for a couple of days, he would play forty-five holes almost on the trot, then retire exhausted from the effort but with a greatly improved short game.

The Actor, by contrast, hardly missed a morning. On the rare occasions when he was cast for a radio play, he had somehow or other fixed it with the BBC that rehearsals and recording would be held in the afternoon. The lady Director of the club, commenting on the frequency of his games, had once suggested that he should bring his bed to the club, a piece of social banter which indicated that in her view he was getting golf on the cheap. Which, of course, he was.

He had once worked it out that golf cost him throughout the year a little over 3½p per hole, and he believed that in this respect he was the only consumer in the country keeping pace with, if not defeating, inflation.

What else could you get for 30p these days? Nine holes, good company, and a load of laughs were surely worth these few coins! He spent on golf, he pointed out to them, about half the sum they put into the fruit machine. And what had they got to show for it? Whereas he — well, his golf might not have improved noticeably, but he knew that course like the back of his putter, every blade and worm cast on it. "All right", he challenged them, "what else could I get for 30p? A cut loaf? Three boxes of matches? Two hours' parking in the multilevel car park? A pint of petrol? One first-class and one second-class stamp? Thanks very much. I'll settle for a round of golf, and I'm not bringing my bed here either."

'IRISH' THE HONORARY GOAT, 'MACBETH' FROM TROON AND THE CARPENTER WHO KEPT BEES

The man 'Irish' became an honorary Goat but not an Old Goat. He was too young. He was barely fifty five. He occasionally joined the others in the mornings and they teased him about his not being at his desk.

"If people like me didn't keep working, there'd be no pensions for you lot. What are you all having?" he asked.

Mention of the word pensions had much the same effect on them as 'cats' on a dog: an odd mixture of hope and dread. They had all worked long years for this weekly hand out and they were only too happy to form an orderly queue for it every Thursday morning at the local Post Office. Thursday was an up day for them. Their biorhythms were working nicely, thank you, and the Actor's statistics showed quite clearly a healthy down swing in the graph of their scores on Thursdays. It did wonders for their game. They were well aware too that these same pensions depended directly on the contributions exacted from such workers as 'Irish'. He was therefore admitted as an Associate Goat, for so long as he continued in gainful employment. It seemed a prudent step.

'Irish' was an agreeable playing companion. He tended to give the expected answer to some perplexed enquiry like "Would you think a 7 iron?" To others, this was an open invitation to sow the seeds of doubt in an opponent's mind. The hesitant response. "A 7? Well, I suppose so, yes", was certain to create turbulence where before there was assured calm.

Without hesitation 'Irish' would reply: "Oh yes, you should reach it nicely with a 7." The result of the shot, whether adequate or disastrous, caused no friction, for both had agreed on the club to be used.

Equally, his advice: "Just hit it straight to the pin and it'll get there" was comforting stuff for a man to hear. There was no hidden malice in it. He hadn't read the works of Stephen Potter. No one suspected him of practising Golfmanship. He wouldn't have dreamt of telling the Canadian that with wrists like his it was no wonder that he could punch the ball two hundred yards and more.

But it was 'Irish' who on one occasion ruined a tight match by innocently asking whether the Treasurer breathed in or out during his back swing. It took the Treasurer all of three weeks to get this irrelevant thought from his mind.

The Canadian always travelled the course with a twist of peppermints or refresher fruit lozenges, and these he would generously offer round at the half way stage. All would partake except the Actor.

He had read every work on the game listed in the main libraries, but in none of these was he told where to place the sweet during the actual playing of a stroke. It was certainly comforting to suck on the thing as one strode up confidently to play a third shot to the green. But accidents did happen, whatever Freud might say to the contrary. One had read of people choking on their own vomit. Supposing the wretched thing stuck in one's throat! Supposing one died on the long 17th, apparently of a heart attack, in fact choked to death on one of the Canadian's Fruity Chews!

Could the Actor depend on his friends to reach down within his gullet and save his life, as well as his one over par card? Clearly not. It seemed wiser to claim a lifetime's convinced opposition to additives and artificial colouring matter rather than admit to the childish dread of inhaling a peppermint drop smack in the middle of one's best round.

From time to time their numbers were swelled when they were joined by 'Macbeth', a Scot born within a wedge shot of Troon's 18th hole, half a century before the birth of Sandy Lyle. He had spent a lifetime dancing his way round the world in ballet productions, finally domiciling himself in Massachusetts. He commuted now across the Atlantic and kept the Old Goats informed of any new developments in the world of US Seniors' golf. This constant travelling messed up his form. In the US he had played to 7 not ten years ago. Now, in the UK, he played disgustedly off a handicap of 22, except on his return visits to his native Troon where, for very shame, he assured his aged contemporaries that he was down to 16, nudging 15.

Macbeth it was who introduced 'bisques' to the Goats, an esoteric handicapping variant which permitted a pair to save up their bonus strokes and make use of them where they wished. Initially, he showed himself a master of the craft, seeming to know exactly where and when to use his 'bisque' shots, but he had reckoned without the wily Swede, a considerable poker player in his Stockholm youth. Macbeth had chipped in at the long hole for a par five to the delight of his partner, the Treasurer. The tall Swede gravely performed his usual three putts for an eight, then brought out his joker.

"Down in eight and we're playing four bisques for a net four. Two and one I think. Thanks for the game."

It was the last time any of the others, except the Nigerian, the Swede's overjoyed partner, expressed a wish to play this Massachusetts variant.

Another associate, the Carpenter, was certainly of an age for full membership. His idiosyncratic attitude to the game also clearly qualified him for admission into a select company. He was the Actor's regular weekend partner and rarely played during the week. He had been in the Marines during the war, circling the waters of the world. What he called his 'Iceland Campaign' consisted of three months aboard a pitching destroyer off Reykjavik making a cocktail cabinet for the Officers. His carpentry work for the Goats, as we shall see, was less exacting and of benefit to society generally.

Most of his calculations he did in his head. At golf too. He claimed not to understand the Stableford system. He couldn't or, more accurately, wouldn't count. His poor vision, particularly when it rained on his glasses, combined with the wretched stub of pencil he equipped himself with made it almost impossible for him to put the scores against the right holes on the card. The Actor would point him at the green and suggest an appropriate club he might use. Then, with a limited backswing, the Carpenter would punch the ball extraordinary distances. It was a constant source of irritation to his opponents that his failing eyesight seemed more than adequate when it came to long putts, a surprising number of which he would sink with aplomb. He had the squeakiest trolley in the club and the sound of his waterproofs hissing against each other as he crossed the green to his ball while an opponent was concentrating on his putt was, apparently, more distracting than a salvo of Ack-ack guns. Playing off 24, he was often 'in the money', and this elderly combination of Actor and Carpenter came to be dreaded by the lithe thirty-year-olds playing off 14 who had expected to be on to a good thing.

The Carpenter was also a beekeeper and the constant supply of his jars of honey at a pound a pound sweetened the oppositions' feelings towards him. But his true skills were called on when the Old Goats decided to 'do something for the Club'. To finance the purchase of balls as prizes for their periodic competitions, they would toss into the kitty ten pence for every nine holes played. This money was invested by the Pilot with an astonished Woolwich Building Society where the money accumulated and bore itself interest.

The amount of their credit with the Woolwich soon became an embarrassment and they decided to purchase with it an Old Goats' Rest, a bench to be placed by the 3rd tee with a pleasant view over two other tees and three greens. The Carpenter happily made the bench for them, and it was duly erected, its feet set in concrete and with a small plate recording their names and that of its 'onlie begetter', the Carpenter.

The rest of the members rejoiced at this new feature, although they wondered who these Old Goats were, for they rarely encountered them during the week. After the passage of a few months, the Woolwich reported that a further £40 stood to the Pilot's credit, so a second bench was mooted. There was some delay in this, while the Carpenter waited to locate the necessary matured elm. It was thought that he was waiting for the timber to fall fortuitously off the back of a passing lorry, as indeed it eventually did, the load being ditched smack in front of the Carpenter's door. But when they asked him for a replica of the first he had to admit that his rough sketch for this, on the back of a scorecard, had long since disappeared. He was forced, therefore, to work from memory for the dimensions of the seat. The result, out of his head, was an exact replica. The Committee, full of gratitude, let it be known that the club was deeply grateful to the Old Goats and hoped that they would all continue in the very best of health, at least until each of the holes was furnished with a bench.

Chapter Three

Shall we join the ladies?

There was a lot of give and take amongst the Old Goats. Laughter, sometimes hysterical laughter, was the keynote, although often enough five would be convulsed while the sixth failed to see the joke. They behaved for the most part with perfect decorum on the course itself. The paroxysms occurred round the pool table afterwards, or at the bar.

But certain incidents on the course itself would have made even Tom Kite or Craig Stadler smile. The Pilot's lofted drive straight into the Canadian's bag, for instance. The others applauded the unexpected shot, but the Canadian's concern was whether he or the Pilot would be penalised for it. The Pilot cut all discussion short.

"I deem it unplayable," he said and played three off the tee.

He might have brooded on his ill luck had he not, at the same hole on the same day, matched disaster with triumph. When he came, a bit disgusted, to play his sixth to the green at this hole, he found it nestling in a small dollop of sand thrown from the bunker with only the white nose of the ball showing. He had slashed at it with the back of his putter, intending that the ball should play no further part in his misfortunes at that particular hole. He saw it travel forty-five yards over rough, semi-rough and green until it reached the hole and obligingly disappeared.

Not a muscle moved on the face of the Pilot at this brazen fluke. He crossed the green, picked the ball out of the hole and said: "Down for six, net five. Beat that."

There was comedy too, at least for the others, when a snivelling skinhead of a ten-year-old, always to be found during his school holiday lurking in the hedgerows in his search for lost balls, was spotted by the Actor actually pocketing the Actor's ball in the middle of the fairway. It had been an unusually long 3 iron shot and the Actor's rage was the greater for the beauty of the shot's execution. He gave chase at once, deserting his bag of clubs and roaring after the boy, 3 iron raised for the kill. The Nigerian attempted to intervene fearing for the boy's life should the Actor catch him, but there was no chance of that. The lad had a turn of speed Sebastian Coe would have acknowledged. The Actor equally had a flow of curses that the small boy no doubt greatly appreciated. The rest of the foursome leaned on their trolleys and hoped their stitches would go away soon.

For some reason he hadn't paused to analyse, it was not only small boys but cats too which brought out the worst in the Actor. It was that same hole that was stalked or at least patrolled by a skinny black animal in the shape of a cat. It was skeletonic and creepy, or so it appeared to the Actor and he would at once reach for his favourite 5 iron and hope to clip it one round its ear with his ball. Not that he ever came within yards of the beast which simply stood its ground, knowing itself to be entirely safe. The rest of them agreed not to let the Actor know that, behind his back as it were, the Nigerian from the softness of his heart, regularly brought with him in his bag a small tin of Luv-a-Kit, and a tin opener and laid out neat piles of the stuff for the starveling.

"I don't get it!" the Actor had once puzzled away at the problem. "What in the name of God does that cat expect to find on the 8th?"

Not one of them had even hinted at the truth that the cat expected to find the Nigerian's hors d'oeuvres variés on the edge of the fairway.

World Affairs, Finance, Politics, Literature and Sex each received a glancing acknowledgement of their existence from the Old Goats, little more. They were all au fait with the dollar-pound relationship which so concerned the Government, simply because the Canadian received his Air Force pension in Canadian dollars, which then had to be transmuted into pounds sterling. For several months in succession, the Canadian noted with some bitterness that the dollar would fall exactly on the day he had to change his. The rest pointed out that of course it fell, in sympathetic reaction to the Canadian's selling of it. What could you expect? Then the tide turned. The dollar shot up out of sight. The pound plummeted and the Canadian was a new man.

Sex, Religion and Politics were not banned topics; they simply didn't figure prominently in the forefront of their thoughts, or if they did, each was careful to keep it to himself. Besides, they all knew without asking what each Old Goat thought of Scargill or Thatcher, the Pope and the Bishop of Durham, Benn, Marilyn Monroe or Nancy Reagan as well as the S.D.P., V.A.T. and the F.T. Index.

The Nigerian, perfectly innocently, offered a small cup he had acquired many years before as an Old Goats' Trophy to be competed for in their monthly competitions. It had been given to him by a girlfriend, way back in time, before he was married. There was some restrained ribaldry at this, particularly so when the Treasurer, enquiring into the cost of engraving a suitable inscription, was told by the jeweller that it was handmade silver, made probably in the Gulf States and was worth at least £150. None of the others had ever received a present from a grateful female admirer of this value and they returned it to him with thanks, but saw the Nigerian, from that time, in quite a new light.

They became adept at skirting round any subject which threatened the easy state of comradeship. They were none of them anxious in the quiet evening of their retirement to stir up controversy of any kind and they were more than tolerant of each other's residual enthusiasms, whether for flowers or racing cars or their own families. The Nigerian was something of a theatre-goer, and would exchange notes with the Actor on productions he had been to see at Stratford-on-Avon, using his son's home at Kenilworth as a stopover point on a weekend trip. He relished the new insight these visits gave into the mind of Shakespeare.

"What's that marvellous bit when Brutus and Cassius are saying goodbye to each other, just before the battle of Philippi?" he asked. "I mean we might say 'OK. See you. Look after yourself'. Stiff upper lip, that kind of thing. But not Shakespeare. How does it go?"

The Actor had played Cassius once. Just the tent scene. In prison. The words came back.

"And whether we shall meet again, I know not.
Therefore our everlasting farewell take.
Forever and forever farewell Cassius...
If we do meet again, why we shall smile.
If not, why then this parting was well made."

There was a brief silence in the bar. Then the Treasurer pushed his chair back.

"See you all tomorrow?" he asked.

"Yes, OK," the Nigerian said. "See you. Look after yourself".

"Wait a minute though," the Canadian said. "I thought we were going to talk about what we were doing this year."

"Doing? What about?"

"Well, are we going anywhere? Visiting other clubs? What's the year's programme? We said we'd talk it over today".

"So we did," the Treasurer said and sat down again.

Someone suggested they should go to Wentworth for the matchplay competition or they could go to Leeds or Chepstow or the Belfry. What about St. Andrews for the Open?

"We could got to Brittany," the Pilot suggested. "Chateau de la Bretesche. Lovely course, good wine. Four days. All in one car. The clubs on the roof rack."

He had brought some brochures. The Canadian had cuttings from the golf magazines. They got out their diaries and littered the table with paper. The Canadian was ticking the events they might go to, eliminating the unlikelies.

"I think we can rule out the Tunisian Open," the Swede said looking over his shoulder. "And the Scottish Girl's championship at Royal Dornoch."

"Where's the Tuckaway Golf Club?"

"In Berkshire, is it?"

"I shouldn't think so. If you read on they're holding the Greater Milwaukee Open there. Why should they play that in Berkshire?"

"Quite. Then there's the Jersey Open and the French Open."

"And the Swedish Open."

They turned to the Swede.

"Could you get us complimentary tickets for that?"

"No," he said. They were still at it when the Lady Captain joined them.

"Good morning gentlemen, I wonder if I can interest you in a game. The Ladies have decided to stage a Mixed Greensome, if the men are agreeable, and we'd like to throw it open, in the first place, to all you midweek members. After all, between us we keep the club going, don't we?"

"Splendid idea, so long as I don't play with my wife," the Treasurer said.

"Oh no, that isn't very gallant."

"It would be if I played with her. No, seriously, we fight on the golf course. Nowhere else but... she'll tell you."

"We thought of drawing for partners."

"Nine holes? Greensome?"

"Couldn't be better. When?"

"The second Wednesday of next month, if you can all make that date. I'll put a list up for you to put your names on. How's that? I'll arrange the pairings. Is that all right with you?"

They agreed that it was and thanked her for the invitation.

"And if you indicated your handicaps on the list too, that will ensure that I can pair people off fairly. There will have to be a little 'seeding' of people, I think."

When she had left them, they gathered up their magazines and brochures.

"You can cancel that booking for six to Stockholm," the Pilot told the Swede. Then the Actor was warned that he'd have to clean up his language on the course.

"What language?"

"Some of these ladies have very delicate ears," the Canadian agreed. "I guess you don't always realise how sensitive some people are. Even in here, when you're playing pool. I've noticed how they occasionally flinch after one of your shots."

"Flinch?"

"Only yesterday," the Nigerian added, "one of them spilt her cup of coffee because of what she heard you say."

"We all heard you say it."

"Bloody rubbish!"

"You see? It's simply that some of us are more couth than others. That's all."

"I shalln't say a word to my partner," the Actor vowed. "Not even 'For God's sake don't put it in the water!' "

"This draw for partners," the Treasurer said, "it could be interesting."

"I don't know half of them," the Nigerian said. "I used to be able to recognise about half a dozen of them. Until winter came and they all got rigged out in woollies and long pants and fur hoods and..."

"All right. Don't excite yourself".

"I wasn't."

"It's a Mixed Greensome, not a Blind-Date Agency."

"There are one or two I have watched," said the Swede gloomily, "and I only hope I'm not paired with them."

"Put yourself in *their* position. None of us is quite the answer to Jan Stephenson's prayer."

"Which is Jan Stephenson?" the Canadian wanted to know.

"She's not playing."

"Oh I thought she might be the small dark one who plays on Fridays. Hits the ball a long way."

The Pilot who had been to the counter for beer now re-joined them.

"There's a box on the bar," he said "for contributions."

"For what?"

"For the widow of someone called Ernie."

"A member?"

"Died last Friday apparently. I don't think we know him. Did four holes then came back. Died in the changing room."

They crossed to read the notice and put money in the box. Then they took their seats round the table again. Finally, the Canadian put the question they all had at the back of their minds. He put it to the Steward.

"How old was he?"

The Steward thought 65. A young 65. They must have seen him about the course. Played Sunday afternoons mostly, and Saturday mornings early. Always played with the little chap with the funny hip. They did know the little chap with the funny hip. So Ernie was the tall one. Used to swing his club like a scythe? Yes, they did know him, although not to talk to. He *was* a young 65.

"I suppose," the Actor said, "that as we all spend a third of our days on the course, Ladbroke's wouldn't give you much better than five to four on."

"On what?"

"On one of us copping it out there somewhere."

They stared out across the menacing course.

"Mind you, if we wanted to perm any two from six, we'd probably get seven to two against."

"Do shut up, would you mind?"

"When's this wife-swapping match?" the Treasurer said, to change the subject.

"Second Wednesday of next month. I'm quite looking forward to it."

"We all are," said the Nigerian, "if we're spared."

. . . .

It was extraordinary, in the days leading up to this fixture, how this merest suggestion of sex, even innocent Greensome sex, subtly affected the play and behaviour of the Old Goats. They went out of their way to appear courteous and charming to any ladies they might run across during the course of a round. There was an unusual amount of gentlemanly hat raising and 'lovely day, isn't it?' They were always scrupulously careful not to appear to hustle or 'sheep dog' any Ladies' four-ball ahead of them.

There was some modification too to their dress. Pullovers with patched elbows were left at home. The Canadian desisted from tucking his trouser bottoms into his socks to protect them from mud spatterings. And in the Pilot's hat there now appeared the small feather of what looked like a budgerigar's wing, quite a new addition to his ensemble.

There was also an increased interest in matching names to faces. Which was Hilda, Dorothy, Louise? Jeanette and Shirley were the Tuesday pair, weren't they? And who were the two stocky figures across there on the 13th? It reminded the Old Goats of those children's parties long ago in Southport and Saxmundham, Bristol and Leicestershire, Saskatoon and presumably Malmo too when they would be prancing around a mulberry bush, desperate to decide 'who they would have to pull her away, pull her away.'

The day of the Mixed Greensome was cloudless and mild. They had all glanced casually at the board to discover the name of their partner and now two small groups had formed outside the clubhouse. It was to be a shotgun start, with all of them teeing off at the same time but from different tees. Both sexes drove at each hole and the better of the two drives was then chosen for the second shot. After that it was alternate shots to the green.

Each pair agreed not to apologise for a faulty stroke. There were bound to be a certain number of boo-boo shots but it was understood that these had not been mishit deliberately. After all, they each of them said, though the words tended to stick in some throats, it was 'only a game'.

In fact a number of purest 'boo-boos' were struck. There were also some air shots on display, when no contact at all was made between club and ball. Two of these were made by the Actor's partner, a quite elderly lady, at the very first hole they played together. It had the merit, at least, of establishing early in the game, the theme and style that was to characterise their round. Maud, that was the lady's name, was obviously a bag of nerves from the outset and these two early misadventures did nothing to improve her mental attitude. Nor did the long arm of the Actor around her shoulder comfort her as it was meant to. They were down in seven at that hole, Maud contributing one stroke (and two air shots), the Actor four. He reflected that had she had an air shot on the green as well, they might have been down in seven without Maud having contributed at all. This surely would have qualified for some special award.

"Now, Maud, we'll put that hole right out of our minds," he said in an attempt to reassure her, and himself. "After all," he lied, "it's only a game."

Maud, it has to be recorded, withdrew from all golf for six months after that game. Sometimes the Actor wondered whether he had been to blame. Filtering back to the club came stories of her nervous prostration, of her month in hospital in semi-convalescence. It had been good to see her back one day in October, though her sporting activities were restricted to toying with a few coins in the fruit machine.

The Pilot had been unlucky in his pairing. Beatrice, or Mrs. T. as she preferred to be called, had only recently taken the game up. She had had a lot of lessons from the Pro., but she was his poorest walking advertisement. The trouble with Mrs. T. was that she simply wouldn't be told. In the senior hospital administration position she had held until her recent retirement, it had been she who had made the decisions, given the orders, told people exactly what she thought of them. Now, squired by the Pilot, who had his own golfing problems, they made a formidable combination, formidable to each other that is to say. It started early on in their joint round when by great misfortune the Pilot put her into a sand trap from which, because of its depth and her inexperience in sand, she had neither the application nor the expertise to make her escape. Where a soft, forgiving word might have come to her lips at this stroke of ill luck, instead there issued scorn and abuse.

"You didn't have to put me in the bunker!" she called across to him. This unsettled the Pilot for the rest of the round and, in the changing room later, he vowed that he would "never play with that woman again for the rest of my life!"

The Canadian found himself teamed with a lithe girl a third of his age who could outdrive him. He thus had the pleasure of playing their second shot to the green on every hole. The men generally prayed that the lady's drive would be nearly as long as theirs.

This was not simply male chauvinism. The facts of life were that the better the lady's drive the better chance there was of the man's second approaching the green with a fair chance of the pair making decent figures for that hole. The alternatives tended to pile Ossa on Pelion in a disastrous sequence of desperate recovery shots. The Canadian was freed from this added strain on his game.

'Irish' had a similar experience, out in the country, to that of the Pilot in the matter of unscheduled 'air shots'. He brushed past the Treasurer at the 6th, his face a mask. He looked so ashen that the Treasurer worried about his health.

"What's the matter?" he asked. "You look terrible."

"Don't speak to me! I've just played the three best shots in my life and here I am putting for a nine!"

The Nigerian, apparently, had met his exact match, a tiny lady with a replica of the Nigerian's neat selection of strokes. None of these, male or female, went a great distance, but directionally they were impeccable, straight up the middle. Between them, this pair rolled out a series of sixes which, with their joint handicap, must put them 'in with a shout'.

The Swede, whenever the others spotted him during the course of the match, seemed to be spending a lot of his time in hedgerow country. His partner showing all the signs of barely controlled impatience was observed to be slapping her calf viciously with her club. The Old Goats knew exactly how she felt. Nevertheless their sympathies were with the Swede. He was, after all, one of them.

The Pilot left the last green rather hurriedly. This was not because he was out of sorts with his game but because he didn't feel it to be any part of his duty to go through the accepted courtesy of embracing his partner. He wasn't going to kiss the hated Mrs. T.

And so they all gathered in the club room for the prize giving and celebrations. So far as some of the Old Goats were concerned, one might have mistaken it for a Fancy Dress Parade. The Nigerian, pink-cheeked and smoothly coiffured, appeared in a neat Norfolk jacket. Unusually, the Canadian wore a smart, grey suit, rather than the habitual roll of pullovers. The Treasurer affected a yachting jacket. 'Irish' had on what the others took to be an I.R.A. tie. The Swede was in khaki drill.

The ladies were in their afternoon, cocktail-hour finery and everybody, except the Pilot and Mrs. T., settled down to make merry. These two shared the same settee, but conversation was strained. First Mrs. T. had queried the scorecard. She had not only doubted the addition on it but had also criticised his handwriting. Then she suggested that there was all tonic and no gin in her glass. Finally she brought up again the subject of the bunker the Pilot had put her in.

Luckily, alcohol solved the situation for the Pilot, an abstemious man, for he ordered a double whisky at the bar, drank it down as the Steward was topping Mrs. T.'s glass up with gin, then took another double whisky back with him to their table. By the time the results were announced and first prize awarded to the Canadian and partner, second to the Nigerian and his, the Pilot was beyond caring that he and Mrs. T. had won the booby prize.

"'sh only a game," he told her thickly, then uncharacteristically winked at her.

. . . .

THE OLD GOATS VISIT THE DUKE'S COURSE AT WOBURN

The Mixed Greensome had distracted them from their year's planning. It was already a pleasant memory and the season of Professional tournaments was upon them. On impulse, they had decided to visit the Duke's course at Woburn to see a world field of Lady Golfers battle it out. It would be a gentle run-up to watching the men later in the season. Besides they had acquired a taste for Ladies' Golf. They brought elegance to the game and it was refreshing, by contrast with the deadly seriousness of a Hale Irwin or a Nick Faldo, to watch the lissom sway of the other sex at play and be cheered by the merry tinkle of girlish laughter that followed some of their shots. It was the romantic, the Nigerian, who had made this point. The Pilot was unpersuaded.

"There was no girlish tinkle from Mrs. T.," he assured them. But he was happy enough to join them. They would go in two cars, the Pilot's and the Actor's, and four of them tossed for who would risk life and limb with the Pilot at the wheel, or the joy stick, of his souped-up bullet of a car. The Swede and the Nigerian won and elected to go with the Actor, though they had reservations about his sometimes carefree insouciance.

He would point out interesting features of the drive to them with an airy hand gesture — a horse looking over a hedge at them, a cottage being rethatched — and they would be required to humour him and acknowledge their interest, lest he turn in his seat to make sure they had really seen what he had been pointing out.

He disliked mega-lorries with noisy air brakes attempting to hound him along. If they came too close to his rear number plate, he would switch on his flashing emergency light at the back. The lorry driver, expecting a sudden U-turn or some other act of lunacy from the Actor, would at once stamp on his air brakes and bring the lorry virtually to a halt, while the Actor raced towards an uphill gradient and put two hundred yards between them. It reminded the Swede very much of the film 'Duel' which had frightened the life out of him on Late Night Television and he pointed out the resemblance to the Nigerian.

"Bloody juggernauts," the Actor commented happily. "Shouldn't be allowed in England's leafy lanes!"

He had a theory — the Actor had a number of theories he liked to kite-fly for his companions — that not only were the routes of these motorway mastadons needlessly bucolic, but that their journey itself was unnecessary. According to him they all travelled empty of freight. To this, the Swede and the Nigerian, both with long experience in the business of Import/Export, made the mild response that, no doubt, the lorry had already delivered its precious load and was now hurrying back to base for more. The Actor would have nothing of this.

"Rubbish!" he said, glancing venomously in his rear mirror. "Loading up at Woburn? To take what where? Golf Programmes to Newcastle on Tyne? I simply don't believe it."

At the outset, there had been some discussion of the best route to take and the Pilot had airily dismissed all other possibilities except that laid down on his own flight plan. The Actor had decided to ignore this and go the pretty way. They would meet in the car park at the course. They had all persuaded their loved ones to provide a suitable lunch to take with them. The Nigerian had brought a ruck sack crammed with stuff. The Actor had brought his shooting stick, and the Swede, for some reason best known to him, a pair of opera glasses. His field glasses must be in the attic, but he had been unable to put his hand on them.

"We shall be very close to these girls," the Nigerian reminded him.

"Not all the time. Besides I want to see how Hanna Linstrom plays, and we may not be following her."

"Who's she?"

"She's a Swedish girl. Very good. I fancy her."

"You do?"

"To win the tournament."

"Oh."

"Do they play much golf in Sweden then?"

"They play a lot of good golf there, yes." "Amongst the fjords?" "That's Norway!"

"Is a fjord treated as Casual Water?" the Actor wanted to know, swerving to let the exasperated lorry driver past at last. The Nigerian, still thinking of the film 'Duel', could turn his head to the front once again. For a mile he had been studying the angry face of the driver. His neck had developed a little crick in it.

"You see! Empty!" the Actor nodded to the loose tarpaulin flapping idly on the back of the lorry. "The whole country's full of juggernauts pelting along to a rest-stop for a smoko. Bloody absurd!"

"Would anyone like a tomato sandwich?" The Nigerian was already feeling a bit peckish.

"Keep it till we get there."

"We're here now by the look of it," said the Swede, and read the AA notice. "L.G.U. tournament. Green badges turn left. What colour's ours?"

"I haven't got a badge," said the Actor and swung left all the same. The trees at once closed about them and they bumped their way along a made-up path. After half a mile they came to a group of what appeared to be Boy Scouts. One of them held up a hand to arrest their further progress. The Actor wound down his window.

"Three tickets please," he said. "And how much is it for Senior Citizens?"

"For what?"

"Look, ask your patrol leader, would you mind?"

The boy turned to his superior, a lad of fourteen.

"It's four pounds fifty," he said. "Keep left, then turn left and it's straight on."

"Yes, but is there a concession for veterans? For O.A.P.s?"

The dwarf in shorts stared at him.

"No, there in't!"

The Actor decided to appeal to the emotions of the stunted youth.

"My uncle," he said, "is well over ninety."

The boy peered into the back of the car and studied the grey-haired Nigerian.

"Can't 'elp that. Next!" he shouted and waved up the following car.

The others passed three pounds to the Actor.

"You'd think," he said "that they'd want to encourage people like us to support the young and nubile at the outset of their careers, wouldn't you?"

"I expect the police have put out a warning."

"A warning?" The Actor swivelled round to challenge this. "About what?"

"Well this kind of event must attract some very peculiar people" the Swede elaborated. "You know, weirdos."

"Weirdos," the Actor echoed.

At this point, the car hit a sudden dip in the path as it bumped its way to the car park, sheltering in the heart of a leafy copse.

"I appreciate," the Actor said, "that in Sweden there is a certain laxity in moral standards. But this, for God's sake, is leafy Beds. We're here for the golf. What are you here for? Hanna Linstrom, I suppose? Anyway, we've arrived. Don't forget the driver."

They tramped a further three quarters of a mile through forest and bracken and debouched on the midpoint of the second fairway. A group of four strapping girls marched past, escorted by scorers, stewards and camp followers. In their wake they remet their friends.

"Where have you been?" the Pilot wanted to know. "Did you come the way I said? We've been here forty minutes."

"Certainly not," said the Actor.

"Your rucksack looks a bit heavy," the Canadian said to the Nigerian.

"It is a bit. It's full of beer cans. Who are these four?"

"Two English girls, an Italian and a Moroccan. Shall we wait for the next four? Nice of them to give us a concessionary rate, wasn't it?" The Actor turned to the speaker. He couldn't believe his ears.

"What — concessionary rate?"

"Fifty p. for Senior Citizens and Infants. Why? Where are you going?"

The Actor was about to plunge back into the woods. He turned.

"Did you come in by the Boy Scouts' gate?"

"Yes, but we went over their heads. There was a sort of pack leader there, in green shorts and smoking a pipe."

But the Actor had already disappeared into the undergrowth. They saw him a good hour later when he caught them up at the 10th or rather when he met them at the 10th, for he had reversed the normal route, following the course backwards from the 18th green to the 18th tee, then to the 17th green and tee until the reunion at the 10th. He was breathless but beaming.

"I've seen them all come through," he said. "It's quite the best way to watch golf. Go in the opposite direction. That way there's only about two minutes between each group and you see all of them, instead of dragging along with the same four all the time."

"Where did you get to?" the Treasurer asked.

"I've been to the Chief Scout's wigwam, or whatever he calls it. The chap with the pipe gave me these for you two" and he handed a pound each to the Nigerian and the Swede.

"They shouldn't put small boys in key positions like that. Now, what's all this about golf?"

They were now following the final four, leaders from yesterday's round. They had acquired scorecards too.

"How did Hanna get on?"

"She shot an 83."

"Sssh!" someone in the crowd warned them. An American girl nonchalantly holed a ten-yarder and the crowd moved across to the next tee.

The Old Goats kept looking for the Nigerian. He wasn't very tall and it didn't help to look out for silver hair, since many of the lady spectators had a similar distinguishing feature. Whenever they did manage to locate him, he would be standing on his toes, not watching play, but obviously searching for them. Then, when the gallery broke up he would scuttle to keep up with the others. He was anxious not to get lost. By the time they reached the twelfth hole he admitted that he had only seen three strokes actually played in the entire morning.

They followed the leaders to the 14th, then decided it was time for lunch and selected an agreeable site with a good view of whatever was taking place. They all agreed that it was thoughtful of the Nigerian to have brought cans of beer, for the refreshment tents were a two mile walk, back at the 1st tee.

Unfortunately, the Nigerian had not removed the cans from the deep freeze the night before and the stuff was still frozen solid. And although he had brought a tin-opener with him, there was no question of any of them sucking chunks of solid lager. This meant that the Nigerian, unlightened of his load, would be forced to trudge round the afternoon's play with the heavy rucksack still bending his shoulders under its weight. If he had thought, he might have brought his golf trolley with him. He was sorry to have let them down, and he offered them some of his huge pile of tomato sandwiches. They, for their part, were equally well cared for. There was a selection of tuna, egg and cress, ham and pickle. There was also rock cake and packets of chocolate biscuits.

The sun beat down gently on them, for they were protected from its direct rays by tall pines. The Nigerian spread a tartan rug for them to eat off decorously, and the Canadian periodically circled them collecting garbage in a jiffy bag he had brought for the purpose. Soon they were lying contentedly on their backs, staring up at a squirrel leaping from tree to tree.

"This is the life," said the Treasurer, and his eyes closed happily. The others discussed the play they had seen.

"That Jo Ann Carner sure hits the ball some distance," the Canadian said.

"And they're all so darned accurate to the green!"

They each had their favourites. Kitrina Douglas as she was British, carried a lot of their nominal money, as did Cathy Panton, Dale Reid and Jenny Lee-Smith.

"Hanna Linstrom," the Swede pointed out, "often has a moderate first round. But she finishes well."

"With an 83, she'd have to!"

The Pilot rolled over on his front.

"There's a four coming up now," he reported. "Let's look at the Order of Play sheet."

"I guess I'll follow some of the back markers for a bit," the Canadian said. "It's not so damn demoralising."

Slowly they gathered themselves together. The Treasurer was still dozing.

"We can come back for him" they decided, and wandered off to join the gallery bringing up the latest four. They watched the four girls potter round the green then followed them for their drives at the next hole. Three were down the fairway, the fourth was hooked into the trees. They could hear the 'clock' of the ball against a distant trunk. It was a long, wild hit but they decided to follow the other three and watch their immaculate second shots to the green. The fourth girl meanwhile was striding towards the trees followed by her caddy and a small crowd of gleeful spectators curious to see 'how she got out of that little lot'. For it was the kind of trouble they were all familiar with. They had made a neat circle round the ball, and the Old Goats pressing through to watch a player in travail picked up some of the crowd's comments.

"It's some old tramp, isn't it?"

A steward had hurried up officiously.

"Leave the ball where it is, please, and stand well back!"

The ball had landed on the Nigerian's tartan rug, two inches from a half eaten rock cake. The Treasurer lay beside it, unaware of the focus of attention he had become. He was still asleep, a small smile on his face, sun dappling his brow. There was some technical discussion of Outside Agencies and Loose Impediments. Or was it a Movable Obstruction?

"Anyway," somebody asked, "what *is* that thing? And was he actually eating it?"

"It's cake."

"Good God!"

The Treasurer opened his eyes and found himself staring up at the bronzed face of the Australian girl. She was dressed in green shorts, a loose green pullover and yellow ankle socks. The Treasurer scrambled to his feet and was about to gather up the tartan tablecloth and the cake when the Steward halted him. There had to be a ruling. The Australian girl was happy to play it as it lay from the rug, but asked for the rock cake to be removed by the Steward. The shot from the blanket was faultless. It lifted cleanly from the tartan, cleared the trees and ran towards the green. There was a spatter of applause at this and the Treasurer joined the others in clapping, until he was chilled by the looks some of the other spectators gave him. He folded the rug and hastened to fade into the gallery inconspicuously.

But now there was another alarm. The Nigerian was missing. Perhaps he had shrunk away from the scene, rather than reclaim the offending tablecloth. But they spotted him two holes later and then pretended not to. It was a short hole, with a carry of little over 120 yards to the green. Twenty yards short of this, just as the Australian was about to take her 8 iron to the ball, a small grey-haired figure, heavily laden, picked his way across the fairway just short of the green. The Steward's bellow of 'Fore!' was carried away in the wind, and other voices now joined in, urging the man to get off the course and quick about it! Finally the Nigerian completed his passage and stood staring about him.

"He's looking for us," the Canadian said, lowering the Swede's opera-glasses. The Pilot took the glasses.

"Now he's brushing his moustache with his hand. He's got no idea where we are, or where he is for that matter."

"Sssh!" said several people nearby.

The Canadian felt aggrieved.

"We've lost our friend," he explained to his neighbour. The neighbour glared at him with some hostility.

"This Aussie girl's three under par and making a charge. Give her a chance!"

It seemed prudent for them to withdraw a little. The Pilot noticed that people were pointing out the Treasurer to their friends, no doubt telling them of the rock cake incident. If now they were all identified as colleagues of the wandering Nigerian as well, the crowd might turn ugly and make their whole afternoon a misery. And by now they had lost the Swede too. They decided to head across country back to the closing holes and to a less hostile gallery.

. . . .

The huge scoreboard at the 18th told them that Hanna Linstrom had done as the Swede had expected, carding a 70 and 71 for her second and third rounds. She was up there with the leaders again. Near the Press Tent, they saw a big, blonde girl talking to Peter Alliss who held a microphone to her. Then he turned the 'mike' to the Swede who was part of the select group. What on earth did he think he was doing? They moved closer and heard Alliss say: "Ask her if she thinks another 71 might be enough?"

The Swede and Hanna put their heads together chatting for moments in Swedish. There was a peal of laughter from Hanna, a guffaw from the Swede. He turned to Alliss.

"Hanna says she hopes so."

Another question and again the friendly chat between the two nationals. Peter Alliss hung on their lips a little impatiently and glanced at his watch. The Swede turned to him again.

"Hanna says she don't know," he reported.

And so the interview went on, beamed no doubt to avid World Service listeners in Stockholm. When it was over, the Swede led the girl towards the Old Goats and introduced them. The Nigerian was effusive.

"Many congratulations on a quite splendid round," he said.

"Oh, sank you" Hanna smiled at him.

"Two splendid rounds," the Pilot added.

"Yes, two. Sank you many times."

The Canadian offered her his programme.

"Could my boy have your autograph, do you think?"

"Of course," she said and signed with a flourish. "How old is the little chap?"

"Twenty six," the Canadian said.

"Ah!" Hanna breathed. "Sank you. All of you. And now I must hurry off for a shower and a change." She turned to the Swede and kissed him twice. Then she ran off, flushed and happy with her game. The Swede followed her with his eyes, his whole face glowing.

"Told you, didn't I? She's a very nice girl, Hanna."

. . . .

At the close of play they were all ready for a drink. The Canadian still harboured romantic notions about Merrie England.

"Let's go to a typical English pub," he suggested.

"I'd rather go somewhere decent," said the Pilot. "Shall I lead the way?"

"All right," the Actor agreed, "but no funny business at roundabouts."

"Funny business?"

"I mean do try to signal your intentions clearly. You know — trafficators, hand signals, that sort of thing. Keep your lines of communication open. Let's try to end up at the same pub. OK?"

"Roger and out," said the Pilot and shot off with his passengers through the surrounding trees and bushes and exhausted spectators.

The Actor kept on the Pilot's tail by keeping his foot hard down on the accelerator. There were false alarms. They would slow down to a modest 45mph as they approached a pub, then shoot off past it again, after a fleeting glance, apparently dissatisfied with its setting or allure. Finally they tracked the other car into the car park of a Tudor-type hostelry and everyone piled out and into the place, in urgent need of the pub's toilet facilities. Drinks were lined up for the six of them and five glasses were raised to five thirsty mouths. They settled down in the low-beamed room to reflect on the day's exercise and pleasures.

"Where's he got to?"

The Nigerian was not one of their number. They looked in the lavatory. No Nigerian.

"Why's you car window all misted up?" the Treasurer asked. He was staring out of the leaded windows of the pub.

"Funny!" the Actor said. Then a thought occurred to him. He turned to the Swede accusingly. "Did you lock the car door when you got out?"

"I always do. I've been pilfered twice."

"So did I. Three guesses who's in the car..."

They freed the Nigerian. It was quite humid inside the car.

"You should have let the windows down," the Actor rebuked him. "If you wanted to hang about in there."

"I didn't want to hang about! Didn't you hear me honk the horn."

"No. Anyway, there's a drink waiting for you."

"Oh good."

When they were all together again in the lounge, the Actor reopened the subject of Hanna Linstrom.

"What do you think you've been getting up to?"

"I was talking to Sweden," the Swede said with a slow smile. "It has to be edited first. It doesn't go out direct."

"Edited? Why? Did you say something gross to her? And I suppose you're meeting Hanna here tomorrow for her final round?"

"I wouldn't miss it."

"You will if I phone your wife. We can't allow any of the Old Goats to stray, can we?"

"My wife understands."

"Ha!" said the Pilot. "Did Peter Alliss offer you part of the fee?"

"Certainly not. It was a gesture of friendship."

"Oh that's what it was! You know, we could get the hell of a bad name if we carry on like this. Scuttling across fairways regardless, interfering with the Aussie girl's ball, then this extraordinary assault on one of the leading players. A fine bunch we must have looked."

"I'm going to watch it tonight on the Highlights," the Treasurer said. "Were there any cameras around when she played from the rug?"

"Three" said the Pilot, "and one of them had a zoom lens on the rock cake. My wife will be very upset about you not eating your piece. She took a whole afternoon making those cakes."

"I think," the Canadian began, and they all turned to listen. "I think that the thing about girls that makes them different from the men is..."

"Yes?" the Treasurer asked. "I've wondered."

"... is the controlled accuracy of their stroke play," the Canadian concluded.

"Oh that, yes. I suppose so, yes," they all agreed.

"And we've learned what to take to an event like this, and what not to take," the Nigerian volunteered. "I mean, next time I'll just take the bare essentials."

"Like a compass? And the master key to the car doors, you mean?"

"Seriously though, what is the next event. For us?"

They turned to the Pilot for the next item in the Old Goats' calendar. He suggested the Open. At St. Andrews. The idea left them breathless with excitement. It was in mid July.

"Will British Rail be doing those cheap fares? Like they had last November? You could go anywhere in the UK for £2. If you were an O.A.P., I mean. And £1 for kids."

"Kids?"

"Yes, you could take up to six children."

"We're not taking any children," the Actor said. "Can you imagine changing a nappy at the Road Hole, in front of 10,000 spectators?"

"That B.R. thing was only for an off-peak month like November."

"Pity," said the Nigerian. "I had a lovely trip to Kyle of Lochalsh for £4."

"Who do you know there?"

"No-one. I didn't get off the platform. I had a cup of coffee and a meringue in the buffet then got back on the train for the return trip."

"We could go for the two practice days," the Pilot suggested. "Or for the final day, when it's all to play for."

"I move that you get all the details for us," said the Canadian, "then we can decide which days we'll go."

"But we mustn't let our own game get stale," the Swede warned them. "If you have too long a lay-off, it can play hell with your approach shots."

Both suggestions were agreed to, some of the more sceptical wondering what exactly the Swede meant by his 'approach shots'; presumably his final six shots to the green.

When the Treasurer got back that night, his wife had just finished watching the Highlights of the Ladies' game. She wanted to know what her husband thought he was doing, leering up at the Aussie girl from a position flat on his back.

"Had you all been drinking?"

"It's rather a long story," he replied.

The Treasurer's wife folded her arms.

"Go on then. I'm listening."

Chapter Four

The run-up to the Open

They had all made phone calls asking after him. A regular player every Tuesday and Thursday, it finally caused them some concern when the second Tuesday came and went with still no sign of the Swede. Perhaps he had gone off for a week's break somewhere; he had been to Tenerife the previous year. Or perhaps there were family problems. At Christmas he generally entertained what he described as 'the old folks'. This description was a bit mind boggling, coming from someone who, in the Pilot's words, was himself, 'playing extra time', for he was into his seventies. But indeed it was his mother he entertained at that time, a lady of 93, but still looking after herself in her own little flat in Hendon.

But no, his wife assured them, he hadn't been away; he hadn't been feeling too well. He still wasn't quite right, but he would be glad they had rung asking after him.

A small gloom had fallen on them at the Swede's absence. Without framing the thought, they all realised that they had between them established a group equilibrium. When the Treasurer was away, for instance, the level of joking gamesmanship dropped. The Canadian's contribution was solidity, demanding of them while they were playing the game to concentrate on that, stroke by stroke. They were each in turn butts of the others' good-humoured attention. The Nigerian, because of his smaller frame, moved with his trolley a little more slowly than the others, that and his imperfect breathing hampering him somewhat. When they tossed a tee at the 1st hole for the honour of driving first, the Nigerian was more than pleased when he won that privilege, for on the occasions when he drove off last, he complained that the other three would already be bounding up the fairway twenty yards ahead of him and he would have to scuttle to catch them up. In fairness though, once this had been brought to their attention, they then made a point, an exaggerated point indeed, of waiting patiently for him to collect himself and his tee and join them for their four abreast advance toward their second strokes. And although they quietly cursed to see the Swede's ball directed unerringly to the bracken, they would have sadly missed the joy of the hunt for it and the pleasure from time to time, of finding by treading on it a total stranger's new Topflite ball nestling snugly under an umbrella of clover leaves.

They rejoiced as much in each other's idiosyncracies as in their own laboured attempts to master the game. The Actor had once hurled his offending club thirty yards into a small sycamore tree where it hung suspended in the branches ten feet up, witness to some imperfectly executed approach shot. He had been a little shame-faced about the incident, but the others followed his play closely after that, hoping for a repeat performance. Every aspect of the game came under scrutiny. They even had different techniques in searching for a lost ball. The Canadian had never forgotten his old father's style, way back in the twenties, of 'quartering' an area. The others favoured the 'random sample' technique, whereby the balls of the feet, even through heavy golfing spikes, could be made sensitive to the merest hint of a small, round object beneath them.

The Actor had as his speciality the recovery of balls from the pond. He had a theory, basically economic, that if you had to improvise some implement or tool rather than buy it custom-made it was sensible to make use of De Bono's 'lateral thinking'. His first successful venture into the world of Research and Development had been the bird bath in his garden; it was made from a discarded drainpipe and an old dustbin lid. The drain pipe had been sunk in cement and then filled with rubble, the lid inverted and secured in more cement on the top. For the cost of a handful of sand and cement he had constructed a bath that would take thirteen starlings at one bathing-session as well as provide a convenient ledge from which the necks of numerous sparrows could get beak to water without strain.

In the same way, he had extracted two long beansticks from his wife's scarlet runners, bound them together with two twisted bands of thick elastic from his granddaughter's school kit and affixed to one end a small, meshed kitchen strainer. At its full extent he could lift from the very middle of the pond, carefully avoiding disturbance of the boxed water lilies there, those red, yellow and startlingly white Rams, Slazengers and Wilson Aviators that had lain there for days, mocking and taunting those players not farsighted enough to have come equipped for their recovery.

Monday morning was an excellent day for fishing, following the two days' hectic Medal and Stableford competitions. It was also rewarding to make an excursion to the pond after a Ladies' Competition. The equipment was also helpful in teasing out one of the Swede's balls from a thorn hedge without suffering skin damage.

These enforced surveys of the pond water fascinated the Old Goats; it gave them the chance to study the wildlife there — watercoachmen, and the Great Diving Beetle plunging down to the depths below to hound and then eat its nearest and dearest there. Golf was something more than a game to them. It was also a stroll in the English countryside. One of them while waiting another's turn to play would survey the fields and the sky and spot a long skein of birds flying in a crude V-formation towards the reservoirs to the North West of them. Duck? Or geese? The others would pause in their work to look up. The V-shape became a swirling, asymmetrical flight.

"Lapwing" the Pilot would decide for them, and they would follow the swing and swirl of the cloud of birds. A lark would spiral up into a cloudless sky, syringeing the air with its thin song. On August days they would be careful to keep their mouths shut as they played the long 8th. This was the hole favoured, for some obscure ecological reason, by droves of thousands of daddy-longlegs busying themselves in a mass mating activity that would later lead to the laying of the eggs of the leatherjacket and to further problems for the Greenkeeper.

They would spot a pair of rabbits on the edge of the semi-rough, small forefeet raised tentatively as they sighted the approaching fourball before hopping back like dutiful spectators at the Ryder Cup into the protection of the hedgerow. Flanking the course were fields of sheep and cattle, wholly indifferent to the progress of the matches that were taking place over the fence at seven minute intervals. They munched their way carefully round the scatter of balls left there out of bounds.

It was a remarkable fact about golf that all over the world there were these beautiful expanses, prepared by man for others to play on, each different in layout and difficulty but all of them offering the player lush parklands to walk with ancient oaks studding the fairway in place of bunkers, or links with the sea spray whipping in from offshore to smack a man's cheeks, or heather-filled downs and uplands. Small wooded courses, long flat pastures, hilly breathtaking climbs to views from a lofted tee over three patchwork counties.

It was this variety that called the Old Goats from time to time to go further afield. The facilities were the same. Some clubs were humble, some grander. But standing on the 1st tee at Minto near Hawick in the Border country, at Crail in Fife, at Royal Dornock, at Newport on the mid-Wales coast, or on the rocky edges of Cornwall at Mullion, what faced the visitor was a wholly new and wholly exciting panorama of grass and tree and hillock and valley, brook and lake, fern, bracken and whinny, and amongst it all eighteen flags on eighteen smooth cut greens, eighteen unplayed new holes, eighteen opportunities to astonish the world and play a lifetime's best at each and all, or any.

A cloud no bigger than a man's hand reminded them, for they were playing a nearby course in the next county, that the Swede was not with them, and he would have enjoyed it. But of course he would be back. Next week perhaps. Or the week after.

They were well aware that to be retired was to find oneself a survivor. They would claim no merit for it. It had happened. They were the lucky ones. They had climbed a long way up. Now they stood briefly and looked back, resting for a moment, getting their breath back for a further few steps. Then another rest. Then on again.

Even here, round the Pool table, there were risks. It was a solid piece of furniture. Sometimes, when the Club was holding a function and the table had to be man-handled into the smaller clubroom for dining tables to be laid in its place, there was the risk that one or other of the Old Goats might be asked to 'give a hand' with lifting the thing. They had no hesitation, no shame, in withholding their help.

"With my funny back?" they could say. "Sorry. Much as I'd like to." There were hundreds of thousands of people all over the country whose 'funny backs' ruled out golf forever. Surviving was not a passive activity; it had to be worked at constantly. Nothing was certain in life. There was no place that was safe. Even the car park of the club had been the scene of an accident the previous month. To the Swede. There were only two cars in it when he started to back out. It was misty, and his windows were far from clear. But he had put his reversing lights on, glanced over his shoulder, seen nothing and — crash! Some lunatic, seeing the car park virtually clear and almost empty had swept in with all the flair and release of a man who had succeeded in taking an afternoon off from his office and — crash!

It could have been worse. There was only a bent number plate and a smashed rear light, but there could have been a 'whip lash' injury to the Swede's neck. The minor ailments the Old Goats could put up with, not even mentioning them — the hissing of tinnitus in their ears or, in the water-works department, such colourful states as Terminal Dribbling or Hesitant Flow. But the graver conditions they had so far evaded as the years succeeded each other. Except the Swede alas.

The Actor finished his half pint.

" 'Do not go gentle into that good night'," he recited.

" 'Old age should burn and rave at close of day.

Rage, rage against the dying of the light.

Do not go gentle into that good night'. What'll you have?" he asked.

"We're about ready to go, aren't we?" the Canadian said. "It was a good game. Lovely little course."

They agreed, and as they headed out of the club room, the Treasurer slipped 50p into the fruit machine. It buzzed fruitlessly four times and then, as the others were going out of the door, clicked and whizzed into PAY and poured £30 into the tray in 50p pieces. The Treasurer collected the lot and doled out a quarter of the winnings to each of them.

"Yes," he agreed. "Lovely little course."

. . . .

The Actor for one had sometimes wondered how it would happen. Life did not stage its events dramatically in the normal course. Certainly street accidents did happen. Disaster could strike suddenly, but for the most part things, very gradually, happened and one got used to each new stage. The blow was softened, very often, over weeks and months. So it was with the Swede.

There were polite excuses at first. Not this week, no. Or next. Evasions and ambiguities followed, so that it seemed better not to press the point. The Pilot and the Canadian, who lived in the same village, were used to meeting such situations for they both worked in the 'Fish' organisation which through the local church offered transport, for example, and an arm to lean on to elderly people who otherwise would have found it difficult to go out for their shopping or to keep appointments at the hospital. These two Old Goats drove them about the place and they had learned from this to respect the pride and privacy of those in need of help. They never pursued their enquiries too far.

He was a heavy smoker, of course. He had developed, it seemed, some clotting trouble. Claudication. Then the threat of gangrene. The Swede wouldn't be playing golf for some months, if ever again. There was a fair chance that he would have to have his left leg amputated.

Then one day he turned up at the club while the others were playing Pool. He had come to withdraw from the Veterans' Cup. There was no mention of the leg by the others. *He* brought the subject up. He even played a game of Pool with them, his ability to hide the cue ball behind the black quite as cunning as it had been. And he was defiant.

"Bader played a bloody good game with no legs at all. So I'd be one up on him, wouldn't I?"

"Anyway," the Treasurer said, "if the worst happened, you'd be able to stick to the game you really know," and then regretted the words. They seemed to undervalue the Swede's skills, which was not what he had meant.

"I mean," he floundered on, "You don't have to go out on the course to play a mean game, do you?"

"No, I don't," said the Swede and potted three reds in quick succession.

"When will they know?" the Canadian asked.

"The quacks say 'give it time'. So I shall."

Then he handed his cue to the Nigerian.

"You finish it off with the black. I think I'll have a sit down." He looked out of the window at the course which had given him so much trouble, particularly with his short game. "Did you all play today?"

They told him they had, but that he hadn't missed much. The fairways were heavy and the greens tricky. They didn't want to tell him that it had been a marvellously close fought contest, decided only with the final putt. After that morning, the Swede kept away for many weeks. There was no question of his accompanying them to the Open at St. Andrews for which final plans were now being made.

. . . .

It was thought to be too far to go all the way by car. Some of them refused to go by air. The Actor's brother was a graduate of St. Andrews, and this contact might secure for them a couple of beds at the University's Hall of Residence. The Pilot had a friend who ran a private air ferry charter service. The Canadian's wife was thinking of booking two seats on a coach tour of the Highlands, dropping her husband off and picking him up again at Edinburgh. The Nigerian favoured travelling by rail, still treasuring nostalgic memories of his £2 trip to Kyle of Lochalsh.

Morning golf at the club meanwhile pursued its normal course, the blood bubbling rich in their veins as their thoughts inevitably turned to the Open. There were pieces in the paper to raise the tension and excitement. Some of the American players were flying in for a week's practice before the competition proper. Nicklaus was to get an honorary degree from the University. Watson was going for his third successive Open victory, his sixth overall. Ballesteros's game had recently slumped but he was still in the hunt. There would be some great names: Peter Thomson, Kel Nagle, Henry Cotton, Arnold Palmer of the recent past, Greg Norman and Bernhard Langer of the present European field, as well as the British hopes Faldo, Brown, Torrance and Lyle.

The Canadian was the first to leave them, in a coach heading for the Highlands. They arranged to meet him in Barclays Bank branch office in the tented village. He should keep back his Canadian dollars to change there for he would be offered courtesy drinks by the Manager.

The Nigerian and the Actor travelled together by train and passed some of the time recalling courses they had played across the world. The Actor spoke of North Bondi, near Sydney, where they would tee off at six in the morning with a hangover of pure South Australian claret. Mists seemed to swirl at their feet as they steadied themselves long enough to aim the ball into the Pacific in the general direction of North Island, New Zealand.

The Nigerian had made a hole in one in the Persian Gulf somewhere, on a green compounded of grit and sump oil. He had also played in Nigeria and the Gold Coast, as it then was. The Lagos club had been colour free. The only discrimination came from the Whites who granted immediate membership to officers stationed there but not to warrant officers or other ranks. There was only one unwritten law and that was that no two Blacks should play together as partners. The word 'cheat' might not be in their vocabulary; but they were very keen to prevent a White pair from winning.

He had been present at the Nigerian Open in 1971 when the American Negro Lee Elder had won with 267 for four rounds. The gallery of Black Nigerians could barely contain themselves as they lined every fairway over the last four holes, helpfully but surreptitiously kicking his ball back onto the fairway if it strayed. The roar of applause at his victory could have been heard in Johannesburg. It was not difficult to understand how the gallery felt. European hopes for the Open would be pinned in an unashamedly partisan manner on anyone, Australian, German, Spaniard or Brit. who might defeat the powerful American challenge.

They changed trains at Edinburgh and again at Leuchars in Fife. A fleet of local buses took the visitors into St. Andrews and they finally arrived at the Hall of Residence to be allocated their monastic cells, usually tenanted by students. The 'monastery' for this special occasion was full of Americans and all the talk was of that day's play and of the leaders after the third round.

"Who *is* this Ian Baker-Finch?" The Nigerian wanted to know. He was leading the field. He had won the New Zealand Open, but who *was* he?

That evening they strolled round the town. The shops were filled with overseas visitors buying cashmere pullovers, tartan travelling rugs, tweeds. There were book shops with every gadget a golfer might conceivably require. The Actor was delighted to see in one of these a ball-retrieving fishing net going, at a 'snip', at £20. It had more polish, perhaps, than his own prototype and he was reflecting on the £19.47 saving he had made when he received a sharp dig in the ribs from the Nigerian who was making a funny face and gesturing with his head across the shop.

Standing by a bookcase, his head bowed attentively over a book, studying it as he would his yardage chart to a hole, was the unmistakeable figure of Arnold Palmer.

"I think I'm going to faint," the Nigerian whispered.

The Actor knew how he felt. The great man was quite still in contemplation of the book so that for a moment he looked like an extremely faithful waxwork version of himself. Then he stirred, twisted his mouth to one side in a characteristic Palmer mannerism and moved towards the assistant to buy the book.

The Actor had had a similar experience in Nuremberg just after the war. The War Office told him that although he had done five years as a Prisoner of War in Germany he still owed his sovereign twelve months devoted duty and Germany seemed as good a place to send him as any. He had been made a Captain and given a Staff Car and a chauffeur and his duties were as a Conducting Officer to escort V.I.P.s to wherever they wanted to go in Germany: Belsen, Berlin or Berchtesgarden. The Very Important Personages had decided they would like to see the Nuremberg trial of the Nazi War Criminals, so he conducted M.P.s and Editors and the like on a series of visits there. He had spent a happy fortnight sitting as it were in the stalls, about five feet away from Hermann Goering and the rest of his merry crew. He could remember their seating positions still. On the front row, by the footlights, Goering and next to him Hess, then Ribbentrop, Funk, Frank, Frick, Kaltenbrunner and so to Schacht, upstage and pretending he didn't actually know any of his co-defendants and couldn't imagine why he, Schacht, was there at all.

Behind them the second row of Raeder, Doenitz and the others.

It was difficult to believe that a figure as familiar as Goering, through newspapers, cartoons and Movietone News was actually sitting there in the flesh. People made larger than life by constant publicity had been suddenly dwarfed into lifesize and here they all were, Hess twitching and rolling his eyes, crazy enough then in all conscience without the additional pressures of forty years' solitary in Spandau, Goering looking round the court as a leading actor might during that part of a play that didn't immediately concern him, playing with his handkerchief or scribbling occasional notes to be passed to his counsel, stifling a theatrical yawn at the tedium of the proceedings.

It must be just like this to the Nigerian as Palmer edged his way out of the shop. If the door had then opened to admit Gandhi, Mickey Mouse, Charlie Chaplin and Karl Marx, it would have had much the same effect.

"If Gandhi and Mickey Mouse..." he was starting to suggest to the Nigerian as they walked back along South Street, but the Nigerian grabbed his arm.

"Just crossing the road! Look!"

"What? Where?"

"Now he's posting a letter. No, it's a postcard."

"Who, for heaven's sake?"

The man at the pillar box had turned and was recrossing the street with long, assured strides. He paused as a couple of cars whizzed past him then continued safely to the pavement.

"It's Seve!" the Nigerian gasped. "Those cars could have knocked him down! He could have been just another street accident."

"All right. Just pull yourself together. Didn't realise the Open was like this, did you? Who do you think he's writing to?"

"His old mum in Santander. Probably scribbled a quick word in Spanish. 'Having a wonderful time. Wish you were here'. Something like that."

"He *is* having a wonderful time. Third equal at nine under par. Mind you, he's still two behind Watson."

"Where are we going now?"

"A drink? At one of the hotels near the course?"

And so it was agreed. They moved from one hotel bar to another, brazenly rubber-necking. In the course of their travels, they spotted Hale Irwin and Lee Trevino and finally a tall dark-haired boy they both recognised from the morning papers as Ian Baker-Finch. By the time they got back to the Hall of Residence, the Nigerian was seeing golf personalities everywhere. In the foyer of the Hall he approached a bronzed blonde man who was leaning against the wall, waiting for the lift to arrive. He was casually dressed in the kind of clothes the Nigerian had seen in Burberry advertisements in the golf magazines. The Nigerian held out a souvenir programme to him and a pen.

"Do you think you would be kind enough to let me have your autograph," he asked politely. "It's for my niece."

"Sure," said the man. "What's her name?"

"Alice," the Nigerian said.

The man flourished the pen and handed it and the programme back.

"Thank you very much indeed."

"You're welcome, dad."

Then the lift arrived, the man got into it with two suitcases and the lift doors closed on him. The Nigerian wondered why he had called him 'Dad'. The Actor looked at the programme.

"Greg Norman," the Nigerian said proudly. "I was lucky, wasn't I?"

"It doesn't say Greg Norman. It says Andy McBain."

"Let me look. Who's Andy McBain? Is he well up the list?"

"He's the night porter by the look of it. Still you can't win them all. Let's go and have a nightcap." And they joined the noisy Americans in the bar.

One of them was exhilarated by the results of the day's play. He was forecasting an American one, two, three the next day.

"Watson, Lanny Wadkins, Hale Irwin. One. Two. Three. And I'm taking bets. We've got eight Americans in the top fifteen tonight. Tomorrow it could be a clean sweep."

The Actor moved up to him.

"I'll back the Rest of the World to win it," he said.

"Don't do it," the American warned him. "Baker-Finch, the Australian, will fold. Disappear. Langer can't putt. Seve's off form."

"He's nine under."

"And Tom Watson's eleven under! OK, I'll take the States against the Rest."

"Does Lee Trevino count as the Rest? He's a Mexican."

"Trevino's our man. How much?"

"Ten pounds?" the Actor suggested and the Nigerian suddenly wanted to hide somewhere. Then they exchanged names and room numbers. They'd settle up here in the bar tomorrow night at the end of the game. The influence of drink began to work on the Actor's prudence.

"I've got another bet. Ten points for the first, nine for whoever comes second and so on, down to one point for the tenth. Again it's the Rest against the States. OK?"

"OK. That's another ten. Let's drink on it."

Finally they went to bed, the Nigerian having agreed, on purely nationalistic grounds, to come in on half the bet with him.

"I'm not a betting man," the Actor said. "But I would like it to happen. Good night. It'll be an early start."

"I know. Breakfast at seven. Good night."

. . . .

They met the Canadian next morning outside the Barclays Bank tent. The Pilot had flown in that morning bringing with him the Actor's wife whose dread of flying was mastered by her love of golf. The Pilot's friend found himself with a spare place on the plane, and on kind impulse the Pilot had thought of her slaving at home over a hot television set and had asked if she'd like to come too. She had stepped off the small plane ashen but delighted to touch ground again.

The Treasurer, who had not intended to go, had at the last moment filled up his tank with petrol and driven throughout the night. He was bleary eyed with the effort and the Canadian was also a little exhausted by an early morning round at Crail. He had met another Canadian and booked for a 6.15 a.m. teeing off time. They had managed thirteen exhilarating holes before an audience of gulls and gannets. They had lost only four balls into the North Sea.

It was decided that they would delay cashing the dollars until later, when the hospitality cabinet would have been flung open. After all it was still only breakfast time. They discussed the bet they had made with the American, and the others wanted to have a part of it. Then they toured the tented village. The Canadian had to be restrained from buying an enormous golf bag clad in tartan. Then he had the idea that the greenkeeper back home deserved some souvenir, and lovingly fingered a water sprinkler that could shoot a jet 75 yards. Only the price tag deterred him.

"Send him a rude postcard instead," the others suggested. At this point there was a shouted greeting and the American of the night before joined them.

"Twenty pounds against the World!" he shouted. After introductions had been made, the bet was discussed and extended to include the other three Old Goats. There was now £100 riding on the Rest of the World in two separate bets; on the winner and on the top places in the first ten.

"I'm in E stand by the 18th hole. I've got a spare ticket too. My wife has decided to go shopping. Who wants it?"

The five of them then tossed for this privilege and it took some time to establish the odd one out as winner. Appropriately enough it was the instigator of the wager, the Actor, who won.

"We'll meet later in the day," he said. "When it all comes to the boil."

"We sure will. Stand E Row B Seat 15" and he handed the Actor the ticket.

The plan of campaign for the day was that the Old Goats would go out to the Loop in the morning, find seats in the public stands there and watch them all come through. They would have a good view of holes seven to twelve. Accordingly the five of them and the Actor's wife set off for the country, a three mile tramp. The day was perfect. The crowds, immense already, were in open-neck shirts and blouses. They were sunburnt and happy that a great match was about to grow to its finale.

. . . .

And there they sat in the stand at the 9th and watched the groups of four players approaching in succession the 7th green, driving the 8th and putting it out, and beneath them their chips and putts on the 9th.

Soon the crowds were vast and swirling like floodwater into this green and that, as now one golfer got his name onto the Leader Board, and another, already on it, slowly edged up as he sunk a birdie putt at the 7th, and had a great two at the short 8th while one of names ahead of him faltered with a bogey and dropped back into the pack.

It was a generous gallery too, eager to greet with their applause well-known names from overseas, or familiar British faces, however far down the field at this closing stage. Player, Jacklin and Palmer had already dropped from the competition at the end of the first two rounds. Peter Thomson had gone by the third, together with the Americans Floyd and Hubert Green. But there was still a phalanx of big names disputing the title: Bob Charles, Jack Nicklaus, Miller, Stadler, Crenshaw and Trevino. And coming up amongst the fifteen leaders were the British hopes: Brown, Lyle, Torrance and Faldo, the Australian Baker-Finch, and with them, Greg Norman, Wadkins, McCumber and Couples all on the heels of the small group of favourites for the title: Watson, Langer and Ballesteros.

It seemed unlikely that there would be any runaway victory this year. Hole by hole, the field thinned itself out, leaving for the final holes the purest gladiatorial battle between two, perhaps three, giants in front of an audience of thousands in the packed arena of the last two holes.

And so it came about. At the first hole of this final round, Baker-Finch, after leading the field for three days, put his second shot clear of the Swilcan burn and just onto the green only to see it backspin maliciously into the water. His game and his round never recovered from that early blow and he began to drop down the Leader Board although never quite off it.

By the 9th, Ballesteros had caught up one of the two strokes on Watson. Langer's putting was astray and although he clung on, he was leaving himself a lot to do over the closing holes.

The Old Goats followed Watson for two holes then dropped back to pick up Ballesteros. Then they headed for the tented village and lunch. They could hardly eat from excitement and wherever they turned TV sets kept them in touch with the current play.

Barclays were delighted to change the Canadian's dollars. The Manager had spent some years in Canada himself and the two men at once started to chat, while an assistant asked the Canadian if he would care for a drink. The Treasurer had gone into the tent with him and he was now introduced to the Manager and he too was offered a drink. They both thought that a gin and tonic would meet the case and said so at the same moment as the Nigerian made his entry to the tent and he too was included in the round. The assistant turned to serve these drinks when the Actor and his wife and the Pilot also appeared. They too qualified for gins and tonic and soon the air fizzed with happy memories of Toronto as well as with the background commentaries on the play from the TV set perched on top of Barclays' safe. The assistant brought the Canadian his pounds in exchange for the dollars and he at once suggested they might repeat the round. But the Manager, his eyes drawn to Langer putting for a par on the 10th, clicked his fingers to his assistant and made a circling motion with his hand to include the entire group of six in Barclays' hospitality.

"I've three brothers away in Vancouver" he said. "It's awfu' guid to meet someone from across the watter. No, no, no. I insist. This is on me. On the Bank," he corrected himself. "And may ye have a fine stay in Scotland."

Finally they all staggered out blinking into the sun, snatched sandwiches here, a meat pie there and craned their necks back to read the score on the Leader Board. It had been dizzying to keep track of the top three but the plot was thickening, and they all hurried towards the Road Hole while the Actor took the American's ticket and made for Stand E Row B Seat 15. He wanted to be in at the kill, and now he sat behind the American who had his field glasses trained on the Leader Board and reported progress back from the field.

"McCumber birdies 16," he said using, the Actor noticed, the Historic Present.

"What about Faldo?"

"Faldo birdies 16. But — now hear this —" he said with the mounting excitement of a punter following his horse as it edges past the others towards the lead 'Norman bogeys 17!"

And so did McCumber and Wadkins bogey 17 and it was now clear that the result of the £100 bet lay between the single American, Watson, and the two Rest of the World players, Langer and Ballesteros.

"Seve playing his second at 17," the American reported, his glasses trained now on the penultimate hole. The crowds round the 18th hole heard the roar from the seventeenth. Seve was obviously on in two. Moments later, another double burst of applause as both Langer and Ballesteros holed for birdies there, and they could be seen now making their way through dense crowds to the 18th tee.

Meanwhile, the huge gallery with Tom Watson was spreading up each side of the 17th fairway and behind the green. The Old Goats were there, behind the wall flanking the back of the green. Watson prepared to play his crucial second shot. He decided on a 2 iron to the green. It was too long and it crossed the green and finished two feet from the wall and about two and a half feet beneath the Nigerian's nose as he peered down on it. As Watson approached the wall, there were shouts of applause from the hole ahead for the drives of Langer and Ballesteros.

And now here was Watson, his face tense but seemingly set in a grin of suffering not joy. There was hardly room for his backswing for this shot. He would have to punch it out and hope for the best. His caddy handed him an iron and leaning on his left side he punched the ball as near to the hole as he could. It was not near enough.

"Watson plays three at the 17th. Not close," said the American. But the Actor was watching Seve on the 18th as he now putted for a birdie three. The ball headed to the right of the hole then swung left and disappeared to a roar from the surrounding stands, windows and roof tops where people were precariously perched. The Spaniard had gone into an improvised Spanish dance of purest delight, punching the air in the direction of the four compass points in turn. Olé! And the crowd as a man stood to applaud him.

Watson at the 17th green heard the shout and must have known that Seve had got his birdie. Now all he had to do was sink this long putt for a four and himself finish with a birdie at the 18th to tie the match. That was all he had to do. The putt stayed out and now he needed a two at the last hole to tie: a drive and an approach shot that finished in the hole for two. It was asking a lot. He made his drive and as it crossed the road and ran on towards the Valley of Sin, at once from either side of the course two ribbons of policemen in their shirt-sleeves raced across ahead of the crowds to form a barrier behind the balls. The police won the race by a neck and the crowds piled up across the course behind the arm-linked barrier. Watson forced his way through the people and studied the distance of his ball from the hole. Then he paced it out and came back to his ball to make the shot. He had no alternative now; he was going for the pin. It had to go down. But it was not to be Watson's year. He got his par four and tied second equal with Langer. And Seve who had been waiting on the edge of the green to see his rivals home went forward to shake Watson's hand.

The crowd rose to applaud a great finish, and the American rose too and stretched himself. Then he took out his wallet. Two credit cards fluttered to the ground.

"Thank you," the Actor said, taking the first bet from him. "It was very close."

"I thought Watson had it at 17," the American said, "till he hit the wall there."

The applause continued. There would be speeches next and prize-giving. The Actor was making some calculations.

"Our boys did a pretty good job," the American said. "Watson, Couples and Wadkins 2nd, 3rd and 4th."

"Yes. Very good. Only four in the top ten though. We had six. I make it a narrow win for the Rest of the World. 30½ points to your 24½. Oh thanks," he repeated as the American proffered the second half of the bet, a further £50.

"We'll see and beat you in the Ryder Cup next year."

"Yes, I wonder though..." said the Actor.

Chapter Five

The Old Goats meet the Frogs

They came home to their own club with a number of souvenirs. There were Old Course ball markers, pitch mark repair tools with the St. Andrews Cross on them, ball cleaners in the shape of a fat thistle. Their winning double had defrayed to some extent the cost of the excursion but they knew they had been a little lucky to beat the Americans. It had been a thrilling final day, but they were all quite happy to be back from the rarefied atmosphere of international golf and experiencing once again the familiar lunacies of their own erratic game.

There was a lot of green on the course now. Rain and sun in equal parts had made for a clean, vigorous growth and the cutters had kept the fairways trim and the greens faultless. The Greenkeeper, a sardonic man, had been applying worm poison to the ground, the scent of which was quite pleasantly aromatic. The Old Goats asked him about the mixture.

"Ah, it's a bit of good stuff that is," he said. "My wife likes it anyhow. Thinks it tastes of Bristol Cream. I must have got the dosage wrong."

Each succeeding season tended to obliterate memory of the ones that had gone, but the Actor as he stood on the 1st tee and surveyed the present lushness and warmth recalled a December morning the previous year, a morning of such perfection that its effect had been breathtaking. The air was like pure oxygen, sparkling as they breathed it. There was a caster sugar coating of frost on the blades of grass and overhead the sky was eggshell blue. Visibility must have been three miles. The little houses and church across four fields and the flat low horizon reminded them of a Dutch landscape. The Actor had exclaimed at the sheer beauty of the morning.

"Look at it!" he said, raising his arms as though to embrace it all. "It's marvellous. A perfect day. I wouldn't mind dying on such a day as this!"

"For God's sake!" the Canadian muttered a little nervously but they all knew what he meant.

And now it was the more temperate, less sensational early summer, and on such a day one could belt the ball from the tee and see it land and bounce boldly on and run and run, flattering even the shortest driver amongst them with the length of his shot.

They played their round and when they were seated at a table in the clubhouse again, the Pilot pulled out for their inspection a brochure he had, and a timetable and a movement plan he had been working on. Certainly they had had a two day break in Scotland. Now might they not complete their annual holiday with a four day 'golf package' tour to Brittany? Four days golf at a chateau there?

The Swede, of course, would not be coming, that was obvious. Nor, it seemed, would the Canadian be able to go. He would have loved to, although his distrust of French-Canadians might well have been prejudicial to his game there. He was a Mason and had risen to some office within that body. He would be taking over his new responsibilities almost immediately. It was all very hush-hush, of course, and the Masonic secrecy precluded the others from trying to persuade him to come. Clearly he was bitterly disappointed to miss the trip.

The Treasurer, the Pilot, the Nigerian and the Actor would be the four Old Goats' representatives in this second invasion force. D day was fixed. The Pilot gave them their embarkation dates.

No, there was no need for innoculations. No, they wouldn't be granted embarkation leave. Each was responsible for his own equipment. Frozen cans of lager were *not* required on this journey. They were advised to brush up their French with a small Hugo book they could purchase at W.H. Smith's: 'Le mot juste' or 'All you need to say in a French bunker.'

The plan was that they would cross from Portsmouth to St. Malo with one car, then motor the sixty odd miles south to the chateau.

Complications arose at once when the Nigerian brought from his pocket a pamphlet his wife had received in exchange for a collection of Persil packets. This offered free travel from anywhere in England to Paris and return. It seemed to the Nigerian that if the others could produce a similar clutch of Persil coupons, three of them would be entitled to cross the Channel without any cost at all.

"What about me?" the Pilot asked. "I've still got to pay for the car and myself to get there!"

"In any case, we aren't playing in Paris."

"Well, the three of us could hitchhike to Brittany from the Place de la Concorde, couldn't we?"

"Carrying our clubs?"

"Or pulling them? On trolleys."

"Down the Champs Elysées?"

The Pilot was beginning to roll his eyes.

"Or *you* could drive from St. Malo to Paris, pick us all up there and..."

"On D Day," the Pilot pointed out, "it was not open to units or individuals to land under their own steam at La Rochelle or Calais as they fancied rather than on the Normandy beaches. How do you think Montgomery would have got on if he'd had to pick up a light ack-ack unit in the Bois de Boulogne and lorry them all the way back to Cherbourg or Caen. Next question?" he concluded.

The Nigerian put his Persil coupons back in his pocket.

"It was only a suggestion," he said.

"It was a very sensible suggestion too," the Treasurer agreed, anxious that the Nigerian shouldn't feel slighted. "Why do these Persil people insist on us going to Paris anyway?"

"It could be because most housewives would rather go shopping in Boulevard Haussmann than play golf in Brittany."

"What's the French for bunker?" asked the Pilot.

There was a thoughtful silence.
"Come to that, what's the French for Old Goats?"
"Vieux chèvres."
"Chèvres is feminine. It should be vieilles chèvres."
"Does it matter? We don't have to put that on the booking form, surely."
"I think perhaps you can safely leave all the admin. work to me," said the Pilot. He could see that some of his party were going to be difficult. He felt for Ike, a few days before the invasion.

. . . .

The boat was due to sail at midnight. By eleven thirty the Nigerian was feeling queasy.
"I'm afraid I'm a bad sailor," he apologised.
"That's exactly like telling yourself you're a bad putter," the Pilot pointed out. "It's negative thinking. Nobody's a bad putter. Do you see that group over there?" he asked, pointing out four middle-aged ladies bound for St. Malo on a shopping expedition. "You could teach them direction and strength on the green in ten minutes, so they'd be able to take on Ben Crenshaw."
The Nigerian studied the ladies carefully. Too carefully apparently, for he heard one of them say "What's that old chap staring at us for? Bloody cheek!"
The Nigerian quickly looked away from the ladies and followed the flight of a screaming seagull.
"Mind you," the Treasurer pursued the lesson. "You couldn't teach them any other stroke in the game. But I agree, nobody's a bad putter."
"The Swede is," said the Nigerian.
"Yes," said the Pilot. "The Swede is." And then he regretted what he had said. "Poor chap," he added.
"I think I might go up on deck," said the Nigerian. "Get my sea legs."
"We're still roped into Portsmouth harbour."
"I know. But I've got this funny feeling all the same."
"Do you get queasy in your bath?" the Actor asked, out of interest.
"No I don't. Unless I stay under too long. Anyone else coming?"
The Pilot offered to come with him and they left the state room, the Nigerian swerving at the door as though suddenly unbalanced by the effect of the swell on the vessel. Up top it was a clear, starlit night. The lights of Portsmouth twinkled up at them. The Nigerian was now

wearing his yachting cap to protect his head from the night air. He leaned over the bow of the ship and peered ahead at the dark, choppy water, as though he were stout Cortez gazing with eagle eye for evidence of the Americas ahead.

There was a reassuring tinkle of bells from the Bridge down to the Engine Room, telling the sweating crew below in the bowels of the ship that cocoa had been served, or whatever message they did exchange prior to casting off. The Pilot had been chatting to a member of the deck crew about the probable sailing conditions in the Channel. He turned to tell the Nigerian that in this man's opinion it would be a calm sea and an easy passage, but the Nigerian had disappeared.

One of the heavy doors nearby was swinging open and he read above it the message 'Crew Only. Passengers forbidden beyond this point'. Finally he discovered the Nigerian up on the Bridge, chatting happily with what looked like the Captain.

"This one of your party, sir?" he asked the Pilot.

"Some trouble is there, Officer?"

"Said he couldn't see any lifeboats. I've told him we've got quite enough for our needs."

"I'm sure you have."

"So if you would kindly see him back to the state room, would you be so kind? Then we can for France."

"Certainly," the Pilot agreed, wondering that the Captain should suddenly speak like Henry Vth. He led him back and then he addressed the others severely.

"Look, if I'm in charge of the arrangements, I want a bit of bloody co-operation."

"What's the matter?"

"Nothing much. I found him up on the Bridge hallucinating."

"I wasn't hallucinating. Felt a bit funny and went to see the Captain that's all."

"Has everybody who takes tablets brought his with them?"

"Yes," said those to whom this question applied.

"Then take them when you're supposed to. I'm not a nurse maid. I'm your conducting officer. I'll get you there and I'll get you back, but I don't want to be seen driving any corpses."

"When do we hit St. Malo?" asked the Treasurer.

"We dock there, without actually hitting it, at 6.30 a.m. We go through French Immigration and that's all. No Customs. So try not to lose your passports, OK?"

They did a little decorous drinking and then they all found themselves somewhere to curl up and get what sleep they could.

. . . .

As the ship approached the French coast, there stirred within them all the memories of childhood holidays in France. They stared now as they had stared then down on the streets of the port, on the busy quay where everyone they could see spoke a different language, smoked another kind of cigarette, wore different clothes, had different drinking habits.

It had been the same in 1939 and 1940 when some of them had repeated the trip, this time disguised as soldiers, and the same in 1944 as real soldiers on D Day and after.

The newspapers here didn't in any way resemble the Mirror or the Telegraph or the Times. And the entire coast was facing the wrong way, looking out north not south. It was a very strange business indeed, they reflected, when one's very Englishness was in itself a cause of suspicion, perhaps even distrust.

The motorists among the passengers on the ferry had crocodiled their way down the twisting metal stairway into the vehicle hold. The other passengers were clustered round each of the potential exits against which a gangplank might be placed for their disembarkation. 'Sod's Law' declared that whichever 'exit' one chose would not be that selected by the authorities. This always caused a mêlée, designed presumably to humiliate foreigners at an early stage in their visit to the host country, with those in the rear crying 'forward' and those at the front crying 'back'.

The Nigerian had found himself swept into this 'non motorised' queue rather as, at the Open, it was the sway and eddying of the galleries that swung him into a position of advantage to see Nicklaus drive or Woosnam putt, on the principle that, as a less robust man than some, if you couldn't beat 'em you'd better join 'em.

During the night he had been awakened by the ship's Tannoy calling his name and requiring him to report at once to the Purser's Office for inspection by the Immigration Authorities. Everyone else had been cleared for setting foot on French soil except him. The French suspicions must have been aroused by this, once they had checked that he hadn't been swept overboard while rounding the Isle of Wight. He duly presented himself.

The Frenchman had studied his passport photograph with scarcely disguised disbelief. The photograph had been taken in Dakar many years before and he would have had to admit, if challenged, that it little resembled him as he now was.

There was no moustache in it, and the hair was apparently auburn. The Frenchman put a finger across the lower part of the face and compared the result with the grey-haired man gazing at him through the grille of the Purser's Office.

"Autrefois, monsieur, vous n'avez pas porté ni barbe ni moustache, n'est-ce pas?"

The Frenchman's English was better than the Nigerian's French though they both stuck to their own language. They had to pick their way through the result.

"In former times," the Nigerian conceded, translating literally, "I carried neither a moustache nor a beard. I once tried to grow a small, goatee beard," he added. "That was in Lagos. My wife didn't like it very much."

"Your wife did not find herself drawn to it?" the Officer elaborated, still in French. "So that you erased from yourself your facial hair."

It was a statement rather than a question, so the Nigerian held his peace. Almost.

"Pass" he said.

"How?" the officer asked, then reached beneath the desk for a sheet on which a number of pictures of men's heads had been printed, 'mug shots' in the police vernacular, some of them full frontal studies, some of them in profile. The Immigration man passed his eyes over these, checking from time to time with the face of the Nigerian staring anxiously in at him. Then he picked up the back sheet of a newspaper with pictures on it. Presumably this was an old copy of the St. Malo Police Gazette. The Nigerian decided to treat the matter lightly.

"Am I on the Sûreté's wanted list?" he asked. The Officer looked at him coldly.

"This is a list, sir, of those considered undesirable by the authorities."

"Then let me clear the air a little. I am not an armed bank robber on the run."

"That will be able to establish itself as the result of our enquiries. Purpose of visit, please?"

"Golf."

"How?"

"To play golf."

"To play at golf? In France?"

"For four days, yes."

"And you have brought the implements of this sport?"

"Of course. A reduced set. About ten clubs. I left my 7 wood and my sand wedge at home."

"You have left at home this 'sand wedge', is it not?"

"Yes under the stairs. There's a cupboard there."

At this the Officer scribbled a note on a piece of paper then reluctantly stamped the Nigerian's passport and handed it to him, watching him narrowly.

"Thank you very much."

"Not of anything," the Officer said and lit a Gauloise.

. . . .

He had not mentioned this interrogation to the others over breakfast. Now he found himself on the quayside and looked around for the Pilot's car. He only hoped they realised he wasn't with them when they drove off the ship. The other passengers were disappearing into the town to hotels and pensions or to buses to take them to Paramé and Dinard. The Nigerian, a lonely figure in his yachting cap, looked about him. Then he saw the Officer of the previous evening's cross-examination leaving a small shed on the quay and crossing towards him, accompanied by two other men in police uniform.

"You are searching by chance for your golf ball, sir?"

"No, for my friends. My car."

"Ah. Your transport."

One of the uniformed men had moved round behind his back and was studying him from there.

"I could be in error," said the Immigration man, "but he certainly has the air. I am only in doubt about the build. But the shape of the face is the same, given that the moustache has been dyed. Confront him with that."

The uniformed man came round to face the Nigerian.

"Your hairs were once 'red chestnut', is it not?"

"Red Chestnut?"

"One describes your hair on your ancient passport as 'red chestnut'. Why is this?"

"Auburn! Well yes, long ago I did have auburn hair. Why?"

"Go. Confront him," prompted the Immigration man.

The policeman took his cue.

"You are not, by hazard, the renowned Lord Lucan?"

"No I am certainly not the renowned Lord Lucan, and never have been," the Nigerian snapped. "And if that's all you've got after ten years' search for him, I certainly shalln't ask the Gendarmerie to help me find my ball!"

At this point, there was a toot on a car horn and the Pilot swerved round the quay to where the group was standing. He leaned out of the car window.

"Where the hell did you get to? What's the problem?"

"No problem," the Nigerian said, getting into the front passenger seat. All three Frenchmen clicked their heels together courteously and saluted the car load. Then the Pilot drove off.

"What was all that about?" the Treasurer asked.

"They thought I might be Lord Lucan," the Nigerian explained. "They were about to conduct chemical tests on my moustache."

"We can't leave him on his own for a minute," the Actor commented. "Did you ask them what the French was for 'bunker'?"

"No, I didn't actually get round to that!"

"Well a chap at the bar said it was 'banquette'."

"Banquette de veau is a sort of veal stew with white sauce," said the Pilot, remembering in time that he should be driving on the right from now on. "When we get back we can tell the Canadian he has put his second into a veal stew. He'll appreciate that."

"That's blanquette de veau, you ass!"

"OK. But it still doesn't make the game any easier. How far have we got to go?"

"About sixty kilometres. Should be there in good time for lunch. Are we having a round this afternoon?"

"Of course. We'll toss for who partners Lord Lucan."

. . . .

The golf course was laid out in the grounds of the chateau. The chateau itself was a tourist attraction embodying as it did four centuries of the history of the French nobility. There had been a brief stain of four years when it had served as a German Senior Officers' Mess, but to compensate for that the Resistance in the area had been active, ambushing staff cars as they sped towards the chateau and the consumption there of stolen cognac, and from month to month blowing up bridges as tanks crossed them on their way to reinforce the Atlantic Wall against an invasion.

Luckily the invading armies had been little opposed in this area, Patton's tanks sweeping down and round before piercing the defences of the German Fatherland. When peace returned, plans were made for the construction of an eighteen-hole golf course among the moats and artificial ponds of the grounds, with little disturbance of the wild life there: flamingos, swans and peacocks, as well as deer, ponies and the great white Charollais cattle in the adjoining pastures.

The clubhouse and residential hotel were discreetly merged into the trees and although golfers came from miles around to play there, for the most part the players were residents of the hotel so there was rarely any congestion on the course. Their first exploratory round that afternoon familiarised them with the peculiarities of the course. It was parkland play with soft, receptive greens. When they got back and were taking tea in the hotel lounge, the head waiter came to their table.

"Monsieur le Pilote? On vous demande au téléphone."

"Oh God," the Pilot said, getting up from his place, "What's happened now?" And he went off to answer the phone.

"I hate phones!" the Actor said. "It's always either bad news or drivel. Either his wife has fallen and broken her leg, or it's raining there, is it raining where you are?"

The Pilot returned in a couple of minutes. He was grinning all over his face. He sat down with them.

"Well?"

"He's OK. The Swede's OK. The leg stays. He's in the clear."

"Terrific!"

It was the Canadian phoning to tell them the latest news from the doctors. The Swede was with him at the phone. They were ringing from the clubhouse. They were just starting a game of Pool. It was too wet to play. Apparently it was pelting down in England. Were they having rain in France? It was great news for them and their mood changed at once. Unnoticed, the health of the Swede had been at the back of their minds throughout the trip. They decided that it was worth champagne all round, and they ordered a bottle.

They ate well that evening, met other guests from France, Germany and America and retired early, for they were tired after the night's travel and the day's exercise. The following day they would play eighteen in the morning then switch partners and play another eighteen in the afternoon. There was also to be an evening's putting competition for everybody staying in the hotel, on the practice green. You were allowed, it seemed, a free drop if your ball ran up against or was kicked by a flamingo's leg.

They all woke up in the early morning, roused to mental Emergency Stations by what they took to be the death scream of the boy pastry cook felled by the Chef's cleaver. But they were reassured when it was explained to them that the peacocks who strutted round the lawns of the hotel always gave this hideous cry to greet another promising dawn.

The news in the morning papers delivered to the hotel was puzzling. They each limped their way through the unfamiliar layout but could find no reference to the current scores in the American P.G.A. tournament. When they had left England, Trevino was in the lead but the French papers ignored the event. Nor could they find any reference to the County cricket matches. The only mention of Britain came in a coy story about Princess Diana's pregnancy, with columns devoted to the child's possible gender and christian names.

"For a nation who chopped the heads off their Royal Family, it's a bit hypocritical to pay such attention to ours," the Treasurer grumbled.

"We too chopped one off, if you remember," the Pilot reminded him. "And Charles hadn't even had the gall to suggest the people eat cake."

"Brioche" said the Actor.

"No thanks."

"I meant that they were asked to eat brioche, not cake. By the way," he went on "I've made a little list of useful French phrases. For instance, if you wanted to ask one of us whether your drive had finished in the fairway, what would you say?"

"I wouldn't be so stupid!" the Nigerian responded. "In my experience my colleagues are always very quick to tell me that it's in a bunker or the rough."

"Well from now on what you should say is: Dites-moi, est-ce que ma balle se trouve dans la partie du parcours gazonnée, ou pas?"

"We should have to let the following players through while we were saying all that!"

"And the Swede would be expected to say after almost every shot he made...?"

"Bugger?"

"No. He would say: Merde, ma balle est encore une fois dans la longue herbe."

At this point a friendly French resident approached their table. "Excuse me," he said. "We are planning a little competition for today.

There are six of us, four of you, if you would care to join us. A doubles Knock out, we thought. Five pairs. One of them gets a bye into the Final. We could play this morning and afternoon, with the final tomorrow. What do you think?"

The Old Goats agreed happily enough, cancelling their own arrangements for the day and the Actor was delegated by them to represent them on the 'arrangements committee'. He returned from his first conference a quarter of an hour later with the pairings and draw. He handed them a piece of paper with the ten players' names grouped in pairs on it.

"There you are. You'd better introduce yourselves."

The Pilot had drawn an American as his partner. The Nigerian was paired with a Frenchman. Another Frenchman and an Italian were partners. The Treasurer and another Englishman were paired and the Actor had drawn the only German in the group. These last two won a bye straight into the final.

"It's a fix!" the others cried.

"You don't honestly think I want to win this competition partnered by a Kraut, do you?"

"So while we're playing off our ties, you two will be drinking I suppose?"

"No, we're playing a friendly singles."

"Friendly? You'll need a referee for that one. And an ambulance."

"Not at all. All is forgotten. The war is over. Forgive and forget," he said without much conviction.

. . . .

The Nigerian and a Frenchman, whose game reminded them all forcibly of the Swede's, were matched against the Treasurer and an Englishman with a rather 'blah' voice who had obviously made a study of Stephen Potter's Golfmanship. The Nigerian's game began to go to pieces at the 3rd when he had the honour of driving. The Englishman, who knew the course well, allowed him to drive from what was subsequently identified as the Ladies' Tee, unfortunately painted the wrong colour by the Greenkeeper's team of assistants.

"I'm terribly sorry to point out that you've played from outside the teeing ground. If I hadn't been making out my card, I'd have warned you, of course."

"Of course," said the Nigerian consumed suddenly by a wave of hate for the man. He very much disliked the silk scarf he wore loosely knotted at his neck. He didn't care for the man's brand new bag and its complement of brand new, very expensive clubs. He quickly counted them and found, to his disappointment, that they numbered 14 not 15 as he had hoped, for that would have brought about the man's instant disqualification.

"You have the option now, as I interpret the rules, of either taking another drive from the correct tee or conceding the hole. And if you do elect to take another drive," he added as the Nigerian bent to tee up his ball on the correct tee, "it will be your partner to drive, of course, playing three."

"Qu'est-ce que tout ça veux dire?" his French partner wanted to know.

"Nous avons perdu ce trou," the Nigerian informed him. "On nous a dupé. C'est un con!"

"Ah ça!" said the Frenchman, shocked by the Nigerian's language. "J'éspère que non!"

They proceeded to lose that hole to the 'blah' Englishman and the Treasurer, his shamefaced partner. They also lost the 6th, 8th and 11th. At the 12th, the Nigerian took a grip on his game and his emotions and hit a career best second shot with his 6 iron. The Englishman hastened to congratulate him on his shot.

"Mind you," he said "with a shoulder movement like yours, there's no wonder you can pull off shots like that!"

The Nigerian, flattered by this, remembered the words at the next hole when he reached for his blessed 6 iron once again. Of course he could pull off shots like that! He addressed the ball, got comfortable in his stance, checked his grip and prepared to take his slow backswing and see his ball winging its way to the 'pelouse du trou'. Then he thought of the words 'shoulder movement'. It *did* look pretty good in the hall mirror. He hadn't realised, though, that it had qualities others might remark on and admire. He came down happily on the ball, fluffed it by hitting the ground two inches behind it and saw it hop pitifully twenty yards ahead. It was no good. His game was gone. He had, he realised, been talked out of it, flattered by a subtle reference to his shoulder movement. Vanity, vanity, all is vanity...

His French partner laboured on, but it was no good. The match ended at the 14th. They had lost 5 and 4. They shook hands without enthusiasm and the Nigerian noticed that the palm of his English opponent was moist. Meanwhile the Pilot and the American had beaten their opponents at the final holes, the Pilot chipping in from forty feet.

They all returned to the clubhouse and awaited the return of the Actor and the German from the 'friendly'. When they arrived it was impossible to tell which had won. The German's face was expressionless. The Actor was more concerned with the results of the Foursomes. He commiserated with the Nigerian on his defeat.

"What happened?" he asked.

"He complimented me on my shoulder movement."

"So?"

"I fell for it, that's all. Have I ever," he asked quietly, "kidded myself that I had particularly fine movement of the shoulder?"

"You've complained about a stiff neck sometimes."

"Quite. A mild arthritic trouble. Does Nick Faldo have a mild arthritic condition? Would Johnnie Miller swing like that if he had a stiff neck? No, and yet I fell for it."

"Oh dear."

"Listen, you've got to beat that English bastard if you meet him in the Final."

"We're playing him this afternoon," the Pilot said with some feeling. "Leave it to me, do you mind?"

"Good. I will. What's your German friend like?"

"He's OK," the Actor replied. "It was a good match. I beat him. Now what about tactics for this afternoon?" he asked and he and the Nigerian and the Pilot got together. The Treasurer, who was in on this pre-match conference, objected.

"Look, he's my partner. I don't care what you think of him, but I've got to play with him."

"You could do the decent thing," the Actor suggested.

"What?"

"You could play badly. On purpose, I mean."

"I have no more say in whether I play well or badly than any of you. Sometimes it works like a dream. Sometimes it's a nightmare. I shall play my best. Fair's fair, the chap's on holiday too, you know. He didn't mean to put you off."

"He let me play off the Ladies' Tee at the 3rd."

"He made a mistake, that's all."

"He thought I was a lady?"

"About the tee. He didn't see what you were up to."

"OK, but I've got his number and I'm trusting in you," he added to the Pilot, "that you and your Yank partner can restore my flagging faith. There's nothing sadder than a lapsed Catholic flailing around for a restoration of his beliefs. But if you bring home the bacon this afternoon, I shall know with absolute certainty that of course there is a God. Omniscient, All Loving and a tremendous all round player from tee to green. That's all I've got to say."

At this the Pilot treated himself to two stiff whiskies. He knew how his friend felt. He had to avenge him. He felt sorry that the Treasurer also must go down to defeat.

The afternoon game started well if a little tensely. The Treasurer's game was off as a result of the feeling there was in the match. The Actor had volunteered his services as caddy for the Pilot, ready to advise him on any counter-gamesmanship techniques he might need to employ. He had studied the Englishman and decided there was no real villainy in the man. He was keen and he played a good game off seventeen. It might well have been through an oversight not from malice that he had failed to warn the Nigerian that he was on the Ladies' tee. And perhaps too he really did admire the shoulder movements of the Nigerian, though this seemed a little doubtful.

But then again the essence of gamesmanship lay in just such ambiguity. You could say to a man before he attempted a three foot putt: "You always get them that length" — and mean it. The man always had got them that length, till now. If the putt failed it would be a triumph of gamesmanship. It was better to say nothing, although even that silence could be misinterpreted. "I sensed you there, sneering quietly to yourself!" It was a difficult game.

They were all square at the turn and the Pilot was carrying the Yank, playing like a man possessed. The Treasurer for his part was the more reliable of his pairing. They were all square over the next four holes and with three to go the Treasurer sank a long putt to put his team one up. One up still at the 15th and again at the 16th. The 17th the American won by dint of hitting the pin with an overstruck wedge shot and seeing the ball pop down the hole like a startled rabbit.

At the long 18th, the Pilot and the Treasurer both got their drives away well. Perhaps it was now that the Englishman felt that a little psychological pressure might be applied. Although his ball was well short of the American's he gestured for the Yank to play first.

"Your away, I think."

It was helpful to have one's opponent play first before attempting to match or beat his shot. The Actor murmured to the Pilot that it was, in his judgement, the Englishman to play first, not the American. The American seemed unaffected by this.

"I don't mind taking mine," he volunteered. But the Pilot held up a hand to stop him.

"No, we're playing the normal rules surely? Furthest from the hole plays first?" The Englishman was quick to agree.

"Yes, of course. It was simply a question of who *was* furthest from it. What does the caddy think?"

"He could pace it out for us."

"Of course I will," said the Actor.

"No, no. If it means so much to you, I'll take my shot first," and the Englishman turned his attention to the ball. The Actor felt there should be some clarification of the point.

"It isn't that it 'means so much' to him. It's quite simply a rule of the game."

The Englishman straightened again, stepped back from his ball and surveyed the scene ahead. He was trying to regain control of his composure.

"A caddy isn't supposed to talk to an opponent," he pointed out.

"You asked 'what does the caddy think?' I think it's your away."

The Englishman's shot had in it an element of unthinking impatience. It wasn't a bad shot but it was headed for a bunker.

The Pilot murmured to the American "Nicely up the middle would do well," and the American duly sent the ball nicely up the middle.

"I think our friend has kicked off into a veal stew," the Actor commented.

"I'm not at all in a stew," the Englishman said.

"No, you've got it wrong. I said veal stew. It's French rhyming slang for 'bunker'."

The Treasurer chopped out of the bunker and the Pilot made a chip to within a yard of the pin. The American duly birdied in four. The Treasurer and the Englishman collected a five. One up. End of the match. The Pilot and the American were through to the Final. But it had been close.

"Cheeky bastard," the Actor commented as he accompanied the Pilot back to the clubhouse. "Still it didn't quite come off this time."

"No, not this time."

. . . .

The final round was played the next day: the Actor and the Kraut playing against the Pilot and the American. The German was not a young man but young enough not to have fought in Russia, North Africa, Europe. He had been born in 1945, the same year in which a bullet had found its way into Hitler's brain, so he couldn't be held responsible even by the Actor, for Germany's war atrocities. But the historical guilt had no doubt been with him for some twenty years, and for this reason he made himself an agreeable playing companion. This rather took the wind out of the Actor's sails for he was unable to feed his prejudices. It would have been pointless, if not childish, to have quoted Oradour at him, or Lidice or Klaus Barbier or Eichmann. Ernst, that was his name, was allowed by the Actor to join the group of people and objects it was difficult to fault: Mozart, for example, and the VW Beetle, Langer, Liebfraumilch.

It was absurd to deplore an entire nation, the Actor reflected, as he took a few practice swings at the 1st tee. It wasn't his imprisonment in Germany that had embittered him; it was what had been done in the name of the German Reich while he was locked away, safely out of it. It was extremely easy to forgive someone his fault. He simply found it impossible to forget. Nor ever would. He would always fancy he could sniff that small trace of evil within a nation that had connived at villainy, or stayed silent as millions were slaughtered in a 'Final Solution' that debased logic and mathematics and humanity.

Ernst approached with his hand extended, and smiling.

"I wish you good luck, partner," he said. The Actor took it and concentrated on the match. They both played well, Ernst's short game saving several holes for them. The Actor's drive got back into its groove by the 6th and the match went now one way and now the other. The cloud of the past lifted and there was no bitterness left in the Actor as they reached the turn.

Golf had this quality of cleansing the mind of all other thoughts except the lie of a bank around a green, the puzzle of a fairway bunker to be skirted safely or boldly cleared.

The bird life was less evident here than in England and there was a subtle difference in the spring of the turf underfoot. It was a pleasant foursome and Ernst was a polite and charming, indeed at times helpful, playing companion.

The Actor was happy to be back in Brittany where he had spent so many family holidays and where, along the coast beyond St. Brieux his brother's body lay in the village graveyard at Plurien Sables D'Or. And a little further along the coast, this time on the Normandy beaches, the Swede's brother had also died. The Swede himself had been through it all without a scratch in five years. His younger brother had died in his very first action. It was strange.

Strange too that in 1941 the Actor's brother should have fallen from the sky in his blazing Blenheim to 'hit the drink' offshore and be washed inland at the beach where he had swum and dived so few years before that. The War Graves people had located the grave and in 1946 the Actor had made his pilgrimage to it.

There had been two airmen in adjacent graves, one RAF and the other Luftwaffe. 'L'aviateur inconnu' as he then was had had his grave heaped with flowers by the villagers, and this had led to threats by the Occupying Germans in the district that unless the flowers were removed, hostages would be taken from the village and shot.

So they removed the tributes by day and replaced them each night after dark so that when the Actor arrived, five years after all this, the village had declared itself 'en fête'. A long table had been spread with white cloths in the village estaminet with a place of honour at its head for the brother of the dead pilot, and then the Actor had become very drunk and had made an emotional speech to them in halting French thanking them. He had not been back since, nor would he ever go back.

Ernst was crouched behind the flag studying the slope of the green. Then he gestured with his hand, to show the Actor from which direction his ball should come in towards the hole.

"Two inches, partner, to the left. There is a slight inclination from the left."

"Two inches it is," said the Actor happily and saw the ball duly swing from left to right in its dying momentum into the hole.

"Well done," said Ernst. "Well done indeed."

"Thank you. One up is it?"

"One up. With four to go."

They grinned happily at each other.

"You read it well."

"You stroked it well. We are a good pairing, nicht?"

But the Pilot and the American took the hole back at the next and they were still all square at the 18th tee. The others had finished their games and came out to escort the finalists up the last fairway. The Actor outdrove the Pilot. The American had a good second. So had Ernst. Then the Pilot slightly footled his third which should have gone to the green. Instead it was short. If the Actor could put his third onto the green, they should be down in five. A par five ought to win the hole and the match, for the Pilot's ball was not lying well. They would be lucky to salvage a five and halve the hole and tie the match. It was much more likely to be down in six.

The Actor noted the anguish on the Pilot's face, regretting his duffed shot. It might have cost them the match. Ernst crossed to him, his face beaming.

"We have them now!" he said. "We are their masters, yes?"

The Actor took out his 8 iron. He only had to loft it high and drop it on the green. A nice easy relaxed swing. No strain. First a couple of practice swings.

"We are their masters!" Ernst repeated.

Something in the words got through to the Actor as he took his club back. Then he came down and through the ball, chucking his left hip into the turn of his body, and sent the ball high and wide and handsome over the approach bunker, on and over the green. A great shot but too long by thirty yards. They all heard the splash of it as it plunged down into the water of the moat, but he didn't apologise. He didn't curse the shot or his club or the lie of the ball.

"In the drink, isn't it?" he said and put his 8 iron back in the bag. Then he headed for the green and for the moat beyond. The Treasurer had joined him.

"What did you clout it like that for?"

"I dunno," the Actor said. "I just felt like it suddenly."

The Nigerian met them by the green.

"You've never over-hit like that before!"

"No, I just fancied I would that time. That's all."

Ernst had recovered the ball and took a penalty drop by the side of the moat. It was a good recovery shot but the American, playing four, ran his up to six feet from the hole. Ernst was on the green for five. The Pilot stood by his ball and examined the putt he had to make.

"This for the match?" he asked the Actor.

The Actor winked at him, dead pan.

"That for the match." Amongst other things. He had hit that loose ball for more than the match.

The Pilot put his ball into the middle of the hole. He and the American had won. There were handshakes all round.

"It was a fine match," Ernst said, still smiling though clearly disappointed.

"It was," the Actor agreed.

"We were laughing, were we not, until we found the water?"

"Yes, we were. Until we hit the drink. We were indeed."

Chapter Six

The everlasting farewell

The days passed, then the weeks. Finally the Open and the visit to France were months ago, but not forgotten.

The Swede stood by the clubhouse window and looked out across the course. There was a slight mist but the four others were clearly visible around the 1st tee. He watched them drive in turn. He would have liked to have been with them. Soon, his doctors assured him. His pale blue eyes, often rheumy, seemed to have water in them. He was wearing a black tie.

The Steward was wiping glasses behind the bar. The young Pro. was standing there, waiting between lessons, and watching the Old Goats as they left the tee, turned for their trolleys and tugged them behind them down the fairway. They both wanted to say something but couldn't find the words. It was the Swede who spoke, as he took his glass to the bar for a refill.

"It won't be the same, you know."

"No. It won't."

"But it was a marvellous time we all had. It had to end, that's all."

He wandered back to the window with his glass. He counted them once more. Four. There was no mistake. He thought perhaps he might have miscounted, or something. But he hadn't.

A crow circled the putting green and then settled on it. They were playing their second shots now, two by the bunker, two through the gap beyond. The mist was thicker and they were only shadowy outlines now. Then, as they moved towards their third shots, they became invisible in the mists of Autumn.

The Swede tried to remember the words. 'If we do meet again, why we shall smile.' That was it. That's what the Actor had said that day. As if he had bloody well known! 'If not, 'tis true this parting was well made.'

The Swede stayed by the window for minutes. He could see nothing. By now the Pilot and the Treasurer, the Canadian and the Nigerian would be putting out at the 1st. Then he turned away from the window, leaving his glass unfinished, walked out of the clubhouse and went home.